Honor Thy Savage

Dymond Mahan

DYMOND MAYHAN

Copyright © 2025 Dymond Mahan
Published by T'Ann Marie Presents, LLC
All rights reserved. No part of this book may be reproduced in any form without written consent of the publisher, except brief quotes used in reviews. This is a work of fiction. Any references or similarities to actual events, real people, living or dead, or to real locals are intended to give the novel a sense of reality. Any similarity in other names, characters, places, and incidents are entirely coincidental.

Chapter One

Chime Smith

"Good afternoon. May I have your boarding pass, please?" I asked.

While I waited for the customer to hand me his boarding pass, I checked my Apple watch. Working as a TSA agent was hell most days, but it paid the bills. Girls like myself didn't have a bright and promising future where I was from. Growing up in the projects in Louisiana was rough. I never had any support or someone motivating me to go harder. I had to get it out of the mud and make it.

When I looked up to see why the passenger hadn't handed me his information, my eyes locked with my old crush from high school. Prince smiled, showing his pearly white teeth before using his pointer finger to ask me to wait.

As Prince walked off to the side, holding his phone to his ear as his crew surrounded him, I smiled and nodded. Then, I messed around and dropped the coffee cup I had in my hand from staring so hard. Thank God it was empty. I shook my head and hoped he didn't see my clumsiness. I was in such a daze from admiring his perfect lips move as he talked on the phone. That man was always pleasing to look at, from his wavy hair to his size thirteen feet covered in Gucci.

Prince had a basketball player's physique. There was something about a tall man that turned me on. His green eyes and golden complexion gave him an exotic look. Even though he was what most people would label a pretty boy, he was as grimy as it gets. Prince was the king of New Orleans, his name rang bells in the street. Yet, I saw something in his eyes that felt gentle.

The longer I stared at his sexy face, the wetter my pearl got. He was dressed in Gucci from head to toe. He was rocking an iced-out Cuban with a medallion that read *Prince,* which was also flooded with diamonds. His thick, perfectly lined goatee had my body yearning for his attention.

I remembered the girls in my class used to go crazy over him. At least twice a week, someone got into a fight over him. Back then, I would watch him from afar. I was too shy to approach him, and now I felt like I had transformed back to high school. I was so preoccupied I didn't notice his high school sweetheart, Lyric, glaring at me.

Lyric was five-foot-eight with a fat ass. What stood out the most was her coke-bottle-shaped body. She had the body of an instagram model and wore the latest fashion. Lyric was a bitch in high school, and one of those mean girls who went out of her way to make life a living hell for anyone she didn't like. Our eyes connected, and she gave me the *I will kill you* stare. Her hands were clenched into a fist.

I couldn't afford to lose my job, so I decided to be the bigger person. Honestly, I couldn't blame her for reacting the way she did. I was out of line. I gave her a fake smile just to clear the air, but that didn't work.

I felt myself getting impatient with them both. The airport was packed with travelers, and I was already slammed with customers. I straightened up the glasses on my face and cleared my throat. Lyric and her friends stood before me, talking loud amongst one another. I was getting upset and needed to keep my cool.

As they argued, I discreetly tried to fix my hair. I always had an issue with staying still and being around Prince only made it worse. Of all the days I could have chosen to show up at work like this, today would be the day.

I woke up late due to partying all night. When I got home, I barely made it to my room, and the last thing on my mind was setting my alarm for the next morning. Anyone who knew me knew I took pride in my appearance. My boss made it clear that if I were late again, he would take more hours from me. I rolled out of bed, grabbed a ponytail holder, threw my hair in a messy bun, and slid my feet into my Crocs.

It wasn't until I was halfway across town I realized I was wearing one of my older sister, Cinnamon's, Crocs on my left foot. There was no way I could make it back home, change, and get to work on time, so I said fuck it.

My coworker startled me by clearing her throat and stepping in front of me to make an announcement. "Ladies and gentlemen, please have your information ready as you reach the counter. We have a delay already because of the holidays. Please be kind and courteous to one another and move expeditiously." My coworker squeezed my arms before heading back to her spot next to me.

I simply smiled and moved on to take the next person in line. "I can help whoever's next in line," I announced.

Lyric rushed back in front of me with the ugliest stink face. "You're not going to take anybody else but us. We've been standing here like everybody else, getting our information in order. As you can see, it's so many of us that it takes more time to gather everyone." She rudely said with a raised voice.

At this point, there was no need to sugarcoat shit. I wasn't in any type of mood for Lyric's mouth. I placed my hands on the counter. "I can help you now if you're ready. If not, I have to move on." I replied as sweetly as possible.

"Nawl, stink. You were too busy in a daze looking at my nigga's dick print in those gray pants I told him not to wear." She pointed at the bulge in Prince's pants.

I couldn't help but look over as she pointed. Prince didn't pay us any mind. He was still on the phone. I fucked around and started drooling over this man, and couldn't believe it. I began to open my mouth to speak but didn't know what to say. And it was all her fault, because I didn't notice his dick print until she mentioned it. Now my eyes were glued to it.

Snap! Snap! as all I heard, followed by a flash that brought me back to earth. Lyric had taken a picture of me in a daze over Prince.

"So, tell me, how should we caption this?" She asked, waving her phone my way and showing me a glimpse of the picture. I was embarrassed as ever.

"No! Delete that right now!" I shrieked, reaching over the counter.

Lyric jumped back and took another picture as she and her crew laughed it up. "Nope, this is just what you need for some action on your page. TheChime1, isn't it?" She asked, popping on her bubble gum like it was the best thing she had ever tasted.

I wanted to grab Lyric by the throat and beat her ass right here and now for this. One thing about being grown and out on your own was, you can fuck up at any moment and lose it all. I didn't want that for me. I had a good job, and the last thing I wanted to do was fuck that up.

Once I pulled myself together, I noticed they had four dogs in a cage. I wasn't sure how I missed all the girls having a pet taxi in their hands.

"Your tickets did not include pets. You will have to go back to check in, pay for the dogs, and then come back to go through security," I instructed.

"We didn't have to do all this the last time we flew. You need to do whatever you have to do to get us through, because I'm not moving."

"If you go to our website, you can read about our policy. Also, when you reserve your tickets, it states if you are traveling with animals, there is an additional fee." I explained, running down the script we were forced to learn in regard to hostile customers.

"Bitch, fuck you. Do you think I don't know you're being funny? I swear to God you had better be lucky I don't knock that cock eye back straight."

"What the fuck y'all got going on over here, Lyric? I sent you to do one thing, but you couldn't do that." Prince walked through the group of friends they had with them.

"Look! I caught this bitch staring your dick down, so I took a picture and posted it on Facebook. Now she's talking about we can't board because of the dogs."

Prince grabbed her by the arm, stopping her dead in her tracks. "You mean to tell me you over here acting like a little ass girl, in your feelings over a female looking at this dick? If you knew your role in my life, you wouldn't have these problems."

He dropped his hand and grabbed his dick. My eyes automatically fell between his legs. We locked eyes, and he licked his lips. "Look, ma, my bad for her mouth and ways, but my crew and I need to catch this flight before it's too late. I made the reservations online. What's up ma, your name Chime right? Damn, I can't even believe he knows my name, I thought to myself. "Tell me what I need to do to walk through those gates with my pets, beautiful?" He said, laying on the charm super thick and he is sexy as hell.

Before I had the chance to tell him there was no way around adding the dogs, my nose twitched. It was just my luck that, once again, I did the unthinkable. I sneezed in his face as soon as the word *beautiful* left his lips.

"I'm so sorry. Here, let me get you some tissues," I whispered.

Prince waved me off as he stepped back to use the hand sanitizer left on the counter. Lyric glared at me with her hand on her hip. "Damn, you spit on my nigga, Chime. Baby, you better sanitize everything we give her. She might give us that Rona."

"Look, I don't have anything. Don't come for me. I've been standing here nice and respectful, yet you keep coming for me." I didn't care how it made me look. I had to speak up. Why was I such a threat to his chick? I hated that I wanted to be her friend back in school. I see now that I dodged a bullet. She wasn't like this back then.

"Bitch, who are you talking to? Did you think you matter now 'cause you work here? No, boo, you get the same rude ass bitch you got in high school. So, get your feelings in check, hoe!" she yelled.

I wanted to risk it all and beat her ass.

"Man, Lyric, if you don't take your ass over there in the corner since you can't hold an adult conversation. Take your loudmouth-ass homegirls with you. Y'all in the way. Ain't paying for shit or helping nobody go anywhere somewhere!" Prince roared.

I watched every vein in his neck pop out as he spoke. A bitch was so turned on that I started licking my lips again. Prince has always had a way with words. When he spoke, shit got quiet as hell, and motherfuckers listened. One thing was for sure, Prince had so much respect in these streets. No matter what he said, right or wrong, his niggas had his back, and bitches obeyed him.

Outside of Prince, there were his two older brothers, King and Major. They were all heavy in the streets, well-known and well-respected. I wasn't sure what type of work he and his brothers were into, but it paid well.

"I will take it from here, Chime," my co-worker said. I stepped aside and watched her work.

"Okay, everything will be back on track soon. I need you to meet me down at the customer service counter so we can put your pets in the system. After I've added them to your flight, you'll pay the difference. Sounds like a go?" My co-worker explained as she walked off to show Prince the way.

"Bitch, you could have done that twenty minutes ago," Lyric sassed, following behind Prince. I said nothing and let her have her moment as I handled the customers in front of me. After taking seven customers, I watched Prince and my co-worker finally return from customer service.

Chance, my co-worker, who was also my twin sister, gave me the okay nod. I'm guessing that meant she got the Hollywood couple straight after all. I couldn't help but remember how badly I wanted Prince in high school. It'd been months since I'd last run into him. When we crossed paths, he always complimented me by calling me beautiful. It was weird because his girlfriend was always around when he did. Lyric and Prince had pretty much been on and off for years. The streets thought they were a hot couple, but I had my doubts.

They had that Will and Jada relationship. Every man wanted Lyric, and every girl wanted Prince. Lyric and her crew had a dope dance team back in the day. They traveled the world doing competitions for money and won a feature in a music video. I knew so much about it because my sister Chance was on the team. They were a big deal back then. My sister and Lyric were close at one point. They were like two peas in a pod. They had a fallout one day and never spoke again. My sister ended up leaving the team and started working.

After my sister left the dance team, Queen and Prince lost their mother to cancer. Queen dropped out of the team due to grieving the loss of her mom. Three months later, in honor of their mother's death, our high school named our dance team after Queen and Prince's mom, Essence. They were called Ladies of

Essence, and even though Queen dropped out, the school kept the team going. They were great.

I would ask Chance what happened with their friendship, but she always blew me off. So, I left it alone and went my way. My sister and I were never close. Half the time, we acted like strangers until it was time to eat. The sad part was we were so close growing up. When we both reached middle school, we went our separate ways. I fitted in with the nerds and geeks. She got along with the cool kids.

That was my whole life. I was the one with good grades and on the honor roll. As for Chance, it was thanks to me she even made it to high school. I was the one doing all our homework while she danced on the team, showing off. I auditioned for the team but wasn't good enough and felt out of place trying to dance, because I had no rhythm.

I looked up to see Chance walk back to her office as Lyric and her friends laughed and joked with the crew of females behind them. It looked to be a good ten people in all with them. They were all living their best life from the looks of it. Prince lived in New Orleans and had a nice house. From what I heard, Prince's mother had it built from the ground up. The way his mother had that house put together was like a dream.

I couldn't wait to escape this financial battle I was drowning in. Life was hard. Right now, I was slaving to make ends meet, wishing I could catch a break. Hell, I'll trade places with them for one day.

I hated to feel like I was jealous of them. It was nothing like that. It was beautiful to see Prince go all out. Hell, I couldn't pay a nigga to invite me on a trip anywhere. Niggas around here won't even buy a bitch a movie ticket, let alone a ticket out of state. I'm not saying I wanted a man for money. I just wanted one willing to work hard to give me what I deserved. If he was already established, that would be even better. I stayed in my lane, but deep down inside, I couldn't wait to be happy in love, just like all my Facebook friends and old classmates were.

I could honestly say I'd never been in love. I never even had a relationship. My ass would be a virgin forever with how my love life was going. I took pride in being a virgin, because I'd seen what these niggas were about. Everyone made it seem like having sex was the best way to get and keep a man. If you weren't smoking weed, having sex, and dressing up like the chick in the music video, you couldn't be down with the crew in my hood.

Chance came back out of her office. "Don't even let Lyric get to you, sis. She ain't on shit." As soon as the word left Chance's mouth, Lyric made her way back to us.

"I guess they just hire anybody for the airport. They got these two dusty ass twins working in here," Lyric cracked.

My sister winked and blew a kiss in her direction. I wasn't sure what their deal was, but this was far from how my sister acted. I'm just glad my sister didn't snap back at all. We would both lose our jobs because trust me when I tell you, if she jumped, I was behind her.

"Girl, did you want to fight?" Lyric asked Chance.

My sister snapped back. "Your time is coming, boo. Enjoy your trip, old bestie."

I didn't know what to say or do next. This was just like watching a movie on Netflix or something. My twin looked my way and shook her head. We weren't about to entertain her ass. I looked at Chance, who was trying her best to keep her cool and not jump on Lyric. It was a good thing one of Lyric's cheerleader homegirls with their crew pulled her away from the counter.

They left and headed to the gates to catch their flight. Lyric and her friends gave my sister and me the finger and said a few words on the way out. They didn't hurt my feelings. I couldn't help but laugh at how slow they looked.

I looked up again and saw another girl pulling Lyric back toward my counter. At this point, she was practically showing off. They all laughed, hyping her up as she turned her phone screen in my direction.

"Your funny-looking ass went viral. See, you do matter to somebody after all," Lyric taunted.

"Look, bitch! Leave my sister the fuck alone! You've been picking on her since high school after you found out your lil' boyfriend had a thing for her!" Chance snapped.

I didn't know how to feel about that information. My face told it all. I was shocked, as if I'd seen a ghost. I wasn't sure if I was hearing shit right, or if I wanted to hear what she had said years ago. I looked at Prince, and he looked irritated with having to come back to get Lyric.

"Bring your ass on, Lyric. We got a plane to catch." He smiled my way before walking off, leaving Lyric behind.

I guess Prince smiling at me pissed her off, because she looked from my sister to me. Her crew looked at me in disbelief. That's when I knew what Chance said was indeed the truth. I can say I got a little satisfaction in knowing Prince had a thing for me.

I watched as Lyric and my sister stared one another down like they were in a staring match. "So, your nigga been crushing on Chime, and you knew it. That's why you and the twin chick stopped being friends, huh?" Lyric's friend, Nova asked.

"It's nothing like it, boo. Look at me and look at her, then ask yourself, is it true?"

They all looked at me, flipped their hair, and left me in my thoughts.

∞∞∞

Twelve Hours Later

I got off from work and the second I walked into the house I shared with my sisters, I went back to my room. After I plugged my phone into the charger, I sat on the bed, exhausted. A few seconds later, I watched the screen turn white, and the Apple logo appeared.

My phone beeped with an alert that I ignored. *Who keeps blowing me up?* I jumped off my bed, and my mouth dropped when I got to my phone. Over three hundred alerts, all from Facebook, flooded my screen. With shaky fingers, I clicked on the most recent one, and my mouth dropped.

That picture Lyric took of me drooling over Prince went viral. I scanned the comments and noticed a couple of bitches from my apartment complex. They were going on and on about how dirty and bummy I was. Tears filled my eyes as I read one comment.

(TheChime1) That bitch thinks she's cute because she's mixed. Thick in the waist but dump in the face. A nigga like Prince would never fuck with her.

That picture was bad, but I didn't know I looked so weird in it. There were so many shared posts with crazy captions under them that I lost count. No lie. I had to laugh at the shit myself. They called me the "thirsty TSA" and other captions down to "If desperate was a person."

I even started sharing some of the shit others posted. I wasn't about to let this shit get me down. I wished I had a comeback for all this hype. The only comeback good enough for this was for Prince and me to end up together. We might even get married on her ass. She better believe my get-back will be me having her nigga, kids and all.

Looking down at my phone screen, I shook my head as a knock at my door startled me. "Yes?" I answered, not wanting to be bothered. I just couldn't keep my eyes off my picture. I did look pitiful. I was so mad I wanted to cry, but I didn't. This was my fault.

"When I knock, you say come in after you unlock the door." Chance called out from the door.

I was not in the mood to be fucked with, yet I knew she wanted to check on me. I said nothing. I just got up and unlocked the door. I didn't even bother to open it. I just unlocked it and sat the fuck back down. As soon as I reached my bed, I fell back on it and listened to her footsteps coming my way.

"You know this shit is funny as fuck, right?" she asked.

I was sure she had the picture on her phone, looking at it, and laughing.

"So, are you coming in here talking about it?" I sat up on the bed to look my sister in the eyes. All this was uncalled for. She knew I was already feeling low.

"Okay, I'm sorry, but I got something that may cheer you up." She made a dash for the door and down the hall. I could hear her feet racing. In a blink of an eye, she was back with a big black bag in one hand and a dog in the other with a cute little vest on.

She tossed the black bag at my feet. "It's for all your trouble with Lyric and Prince."

I unzipped the bag and lost my breath as I pulled out all the money. For some reason, I got hot as hell and jumped up and raced to the bathroom. I splashed water in my eyes to make sure I wasn't dreaming. Today had already been a hell of a day. That's when it hit me. She had done her credit card scheme. I hoped to God it wasn't on Prince, because that nigga was crazy in the streets. The dog she had sure looked like the one Lyric had in the pet taxi.

Please don't let her have done what I think she did. Prince wasn't the type of nigga who would hesitate to bring heat to our door. As I stared at her, my stomach twisted in a knot as I prayed she didn't do the unthinkable again.

Chapter Two

Prince Brown

A nigga didn't even have a chance to sit in his seat before the Lyric started her shit. I played it to the left and ignored the first shot she took at me. Knowing how Lyric's words could hurt a nigga's pride, I let her have her moment. She needed it more than I did. If she knew how much money she could make if she applied that mouth to her own business, she'd be good.

Everyone else's life was more important, or should I say more interesting, than her own. My biggest turnoff was her mouth. She didn't know how or when to just be quiet. There were times I had to remind Lyric of who the fuck I was. I got respect from everyone but her, which was about to change.

"Just go sit the fuck down and shut up. You're doing too much. Try to be happy for a chance. Let your hair down on this free-ass trip. You got it made to be on a trip with all your close friends, but somehow this still isn't enough."

"Why do you always do that? Does it make you feel good saying what you do for me?" she asked.

I wasn't feeling this conversation with Lyric. That showing out in public shit was getting old with us. It was at the top of my 'don't do list', and she'd been fucking with a nigga long enough to know. Nowadays, I could say everything about us was getting old. A nigga had been ready to throw the towel in. It was time to move on any time you felt like being with a person was breaking you.

I never thought things would get this bad. The flame we had

back in high school was gone. When we first met, Lyric and I were cool. There were no titles or strings attached. Then, when a nigga got locked up, she held me down. So, I felt, and still feel, obligated to be with her. I caught a little gun charge, and also had a quarter pound of weed on me, back in the day. Nothing about what she did was easy. We had a lot of history between us.

Shawty held it down while I got locked up and kept shit hot. Lyric sending me money and trapping for a nigga was enough for me. I had to pull some time, and the day I got sentenced, Lyric told me she was pregnant. My entire world changed when she told me that. It gave me life, and I was looking forward to getting home.

Lyric came to visit me after she delivered our child to tell me the baby was stillborn. That same night I got my daughter's name, Harmony, tattooed on my right arm with her birthdate under it, saying '*daddy's little girl*'. That alone was why I stayed with Lyric. She was the mother of my first child. I wanted a baby bad as hell back then. However, losing her only made me take it as a sign we weren't ready.

"I see you're frustrated, so I'll let you have this moment. Besides, I love you and appreciate everything you do." Lyric said, kissing me as she sat down and buckled herself in.

Within minutes, our flight took off. I closed my eyes and hoped this sale would go as planned. As I thought about the details of this trip, I felt my pants being pulled on.

"Let me please him for you, baby." Lyric cooed with her travel blanket over her head in my lap. She unzipped my pants, which everyone could hear in the next two rows. Not that I gave a fuck. Shawty was right on time.

As soon as I felt her lips touch my dick, I jumped. I relaxed and let her do her thing. Lyric took my dick in her mouth, using her tongue to lick and suck the head of my shit. My eyes rolled into the back of my head. She went straight for my balls in a circular motion, which she knew drove a nigga insane. It had a nigga doing stretches on the flight. No cap. Shawty started doing tricks with her tongue that had me pat her on the back when she was done. A nigga needed that stress reliever.

Lyric fixed herself and sat up in her seat. I had a lot on my mind and didn't know why. This was a big day for me. For some reason, I felt something would go wrong somewhere. I just didn't know where. I was into so much shit I couldn't tell if I was coming or going.

My brothers and I kept my sister out of the way as we trapped heavily out here. We pretty much owned everything there was to own that could make money, from car dealerships to strip clubs, and restaurants. You name it, I might own that shit already, or be in the process of opening it. Those were coverups for the real shit we were doing behind closed doors. We'd been slanging dope for the last five years, pushing powder and crystal meth. This shit didn't just start with us, my father and my grandfather started this family business.

Once they left this green earth, we picked it up from there. My brothers and I all had our ways of doing things. We each took over two cities and split the projects in New Orleans. My brother King and I had most of the property since we put in more footwork. At twenty-two years old, I had a lot to be thankful for.

I was young and getting it and got it on my own. Yeah, my dad and grandfather passed down what they had, but it cost us when we got the shit back on the streets, not just in money, but in time as well. We couldn't start the organization back up until we figured shit out. We didn't have any other family members to show us the way, so we had to get up to speed quickly.

All we had was my grandmother, but she had been put away in a mental facility for years. I'm not sure what happened to her, but I knew she had changed. I still made it a point to visit her when I was on her side of town. I also took her food and kept money on her books. Hell, I'd been helping her out since I was fifteen when I got my first part-time job.

Still, she doesn't even remember me. She calls me Winnie. Whomever the fuck that was always seemed to make her smile. So, I never said a word. I just played right along. It didn't help that my grandmother has always been my weakness, so seeing her like that only fucked a nigga's head up mentally. I let my mind race as I closed my eyes to get my rest.

Being held up at the airport with Lyric going back and forth with Chime and her sister took a lot of our time. I had two missions while on this trip. The first was to meet up with my partner, so we could add the dogs I had with me to my breeding list. After that, I had to meet with Lexx. My brother Major and I had been breeding pitbulls for years, so a nigga opened up shop and started breeding pits for a side hustle. We left my sister, Queen, the head of that operation, and I was pleased with the outcome. She had other business to handle today, otherwise, she'd be here rolling with us.

Even though I trusted my sister, it didn't stop me from having my shit wired down. I had video cameras inside and out, so if any funny shit went down, I would be on game. I checked on my businesses from my phone, ensuring my operations were running properly. Then I sent out text messages to all my clients, checking in and making sure things were cool on their end.

The last call I made was to Lexx, and I hated this look we were giving him. I was never known to be late. I answered the call and got straight to the point.

"We made it to New York. My plane is just arriving, but trust me, my money is good if the product is good." I put him on FaceTime to let the nosy motherfucker see that I was already off the plane. He needed to know I wasn't running a game on him. I didn't do business that way or mess with anyone messy.

My brothers were shown to him, so he would see how serious we were. It was not that serious, just out of respect for our business. I was taught a long time ago to never play with a motherfucker's time or money. No matter how much money I made, I never got careless in the game or comfortable. Too much money was invested in my product to play around with these niggas.

I built my shit from the ground up. Blood, sweat, and tears went into this operation. The last thing a nigga like me was trying to do was play out here. Niggas knew I wasn't to be fucked with, and those who knew me knew I worked the long and hard way for what I got. Nobody could ever say they gave me anything. Couldn't a soul alive say I begged a nigga for shit or asked them for help with anything.

A nigga like me would rather rob you to get it. It was nothing for me. That struggle shit wasn't in my blood. My pride wouldn't let me ask my very own family for help. Yet I was the opposite when other people needed help. Anyone could come to me, and I'd look out. I had too much of a good heart. In that same breath, I was a motherfucker. That's why I hated it for those who would try me. I hated thieves. I worked for mine and felt every man should. My mother raised me right before she passed. A nigga like me was hard to come by. I was built differently.

As a man, you had to get up and go get it. In my world, there will never be a handout. Even when putting a nigga on, I wanted it back. It was always something in it. I came up the hard way. From sunup to sundown, I had to get it. Anything in the way or stopping me, I took out. I made it very clear what I was and wasn't about. Niggas thought since my father and grandfather were the old kingpins, what I had was from them. It was nothing like that. A nigga didn't get to enjoy the fruits of that labor until I worked for my own.

Back in school, I was too young to know the value of it. Once I started hitting the streets, shit changed. I got locked up and sent away for two years right after I turned nineteen. That's when the real challenge came. You find out who is down for you when you are down. I can count on my hand who I'd heard from. At first, the love was real. I heard niggas on Facebook were showing love. Then came the letters and pictures, but it all stopped in the blink of an eye. It came to the point where I thought motherfuckers had died. The hood got so quiet on me that I thought they knew something I didn't. That's when the rumors started.

"Baby, I got our bags. Can you get my pet taxi?" Lyric asked, breaking my thoughts.

I shook my head because we had other arrangements. All the females were to carry the pet taxis. I grabbed our things and luggage from her and walked her to where she needed to be.

"Hello, are you checking a pet out?" The receptionist asked.

Lyric nodded and gave the lady her pet ticket. The receptionist smiled and went looking for our dog. It had been five-ten minutes, and my hands were sweating. It was like she couldn't find it. I looked over at Lyric, who looked the same way I did. We both were lost. That's when the lady came back with nothing in her hand.

"Yes, ma'am, I'm sorry. I don't have this ticket number back here. Perhaps it was left behind or checked out by someone else?" The bitch said.

"How is it even possible for someone else to check out my property without you knowing?" I roared.

"Just keep your cool. We will do our best to find out what happened. Please leave us your name and number and give us time," she instructed.

Lyric looked lost but wrote her name and number down as she was told. I started sweating bullets, trying to understand what the fuck went wrong. Could my dog have been left or checked out? Who knows, but they better find it and fast? I got the rest of our things and left the airport. As soon as I got outside, my brothers were pulling up. I threw our stuff in the trunk and hopped into the car.

My phone rang before I could mention our missing dog. It was Lexx.

∞∞∞

"Tell me about yourself and why I should do business with you, young Prince." Lexx said while we exchanged money and product.

I waited until I had my work in my hand before saying a word. We can do this prep talk later. We were in a room full of goons. But to me, they didn't stand a chance against my brothers and me. After being in this bitch for two hours and hearing everyone's life story, I looked around the room and was ready to go.

It was my turn to tell this man why I chose this life, but just like him, it was all I knew and probably will be the death of me. Once I handed over the bags to my brothers, I sat down and started my story for these niggas.

"I have been out this bitch on my own, me and my brothers. I came up and brought the niggas I was hungry with, with me. I put a team of real hustlers in the game, shaping and molding the niggas. I'm not saying this lifestyle was the best thing hitting, but it was all I knew by the time I turned sixteen. My family was the only thing that mattered to me. So, I went hard for them and made it where I needed to be. I had set up shop in four different locations.

"I was that nigga who was well respected. I made sure my people were straight and holding it down before making any other moves. Once those traps started jumping in my four locations, I became the kingpin in eleven months, tops. I put eighty niggas on without hesitation. Some niggas I knew, others I've never heard of but gave them a chance anyway.

"I didn't care what you did. I had a job for you. A nigga was good with the respect alone, and the power I gained. A few years went by, and niggas around me got jealous and started hating on what I had and how fast I got it. See, I didn't get why niggas watched other niggas' plates.

"I separated my crew by colors, and that caused all types of niggas to get mad. Still, I started a wave, and niggas were mad. We weren't a gang, just a small movement. Each person in each group had a duty to handle. I had a pair of eyes on each team, which usually was a bitch. The female on the team is called a go-getter. She was the one I sent in to check on things when I needed to know what was what. I had a money man on each team, which only required one person. I didn't need too many niggas touching or handling my money. Each team had a true shoota and runner.

"I had shit all figured out, and the hood knew it. When niggas wanted to try me, they thought twice about it. I had two different clean-up crews, and all eighty members on my team were trained to go. I took what I needed and grew from what I had. I had a solid team, and that's where most of the hate came from. There were niggas who didn't like my growth, which motivated me. I was young, good-looking, and getting it. I even made some of my so-called close friends and family mad, which was the main reason I stayed prayed up and strapped up."

When I stopped talking, niggas nodded in agreement. I didn't need any approval, but they knew how I was coming. As I stood and walked out, Lexx shook me and my brother's hands. That's when I locked eyes with the last two niggas I wanted to see: my dad's brother, Uncle Peanut, and my little cousin Slime.

My brothers both mean-mugged them and headed out the door. We reached the car and started to leave but got cut off by two vehicles in front of us. One was a black, 2022 BMW with midnight tints. The other was a tinted Bentley from the same year. I pulled my gun out and flashed my headlights.

Two guys got out with two duffel bags. I jumped out with my gun, knowing it had to be Lexx's people.

"Lexx says accept these as a gift from him." A man relayed as they left the bags and pulled off.

We got out fast, grabbed that shit up, and headed out.

"What the fuck was Peanut and Slime doing here? Last time I checked, we owed them niggas some attention!" Major roared.

Peanut and his son were on some other shit, so they got put out of the family. After money kept getting taken and was put on me, I stopped trying. Slime and I couldn't get along for shit. He was always at war or in competition with me for no reason. I was raised to get this shit together. Slime, on the other hand, wanted to get credit for it all. He didn't want anything but what I had, and I never knew why.

To keep the peace between Slime and me, I kept my distance. Then, my brother and Peanut got into it. Major beat the hell outta him for setting my dad up. My brother and uncle were alright until he overheard him talking about having my dad robbed.

My brother damn near killed my uncle, and that was the last we heard from him. He didn't even come to my dad's funeral. Hell, he didn't even come to my grandfather, his own dad's funeral.

"Chill out, nigga! We just got to know how to move now!" King roared at Major.

That didn't keep Major settling for shit. We had enough on our plate, though. The only move I was on next would be getting back my missing dog. They had forty thousand dollars' worth of product on them, so I needed answers. Good thing I had a tracking device on them cause the airport wasn't any help. A nigga would have been caught red-handed had it not been for my right-hand man, Chase Bolden. He is the head of security in this bitch. It was good to have niggas like him on the payroll.

While thinking about getting my dog back from the airport, I kept seeing shawty's face from earlier. Chime's ass was bad and my type. Her twin sister, Chance, used to be tight with Lyric back in school. Now, they wouldn't even speak to one another. I didn't know what I had walked into with Lyric and Chime. Lyric had been picking on her since grade school. A nigga is always behind chicks' beef, so I was sure I was responsible for her not liking her.

Lyric and I had a conversation about who was my type, and I told her if she and I didn't work out, I would start dating Chime. She laughed in my face, not thinking I was serious. Once she saw I wasn't playing, shawty went off on me and found a way to stop being friends with Chance. The same week I told Lyric about my crush on Chime, she made up some imaginary beef in her head with Chance. Only it didn't go Lyric's way.

Shit went left with Chance because her mouth matched Lyric's mouth. Back then, Chance and Lyric were like white on rice. Hell, they could have passed as twins. You couldn't pull the two apart for anything and wouldn't try. They did everything together and even dressed up as besties did.

Even though Chance and Chime were identical twins, their personalities made them look completely different. They grew up to be the opposite of one another. Chance stood five-foot-five and was slim. She kept her hair in a bob, which was sexy on her. She was just mouthy as hell. Chance also dressed her ass off. As for Chime, she didn't care too much about looks, clothes, or hair. Even though she did makeup, you would never see her wear it. I remember that much from her doing the girls around the way makeup for prom.

Makeup or not, Chime was sexy as fuck to a nigga like me. I was attracted to her no matter what she wore or how her hair was laid. I saw past her plain look and saw her beauty. Her long jet-black hair and those gray eyes had a nigga hooked. I couldn't believe I had been crushing on this girl for years, and she never knew. I made it a point to tell her how beautiful she was no matter where I saw her.

She probably thought a nigga wasn't shit, because I did too much name-calling in school. I got the chance to talk shit to Chime because after I told Lyric I had a crush on Chime, she was always around, giving me no choice but to pick on Chime to throw my girl off. On the real, a nigga couldn't tell you what it was about this girl, but I wanted her. Chime was thick in all the right places, making her stand out. Those lips and eyes had me sold for life.

I sat back and rode to the hotel, trying to shake shawty off my mind. It was hard. I wanted to see her again.

As we pulled up to the hotel, I checked our surroundings while King parked. My brothers took the bags we got from Lexx. Nothing but money was in the first bag. It looked to be about fifty thousand dollars. One of the other bags had an army machine gun in it. The shit was too heavy to carry, so I had to toss the shit over my shoulder. I wasn't sure what made Lexx give me a gift, but I didn't mind it. My phone started ringing as we approached the hotel. It was my runner. I hoped like hell she had the information I needed.

"Talk to me," I instructed.

"So, I found the dog from the tracking device. And it looks like one of the girls from the airport took it. I have their address and phone number coming to you in an email."

"You talking about the twins from the airport?" I questioned, knowing damn well these hoes weren't getting at me like that.

"Yes, those are the twins. Oh, your account that you used to pay for this trip came up short. It's missing $250,000, and that's all I got for you right now."

After hanging up, I made a few phone calls. A nigga was on his way to that address. This changed everything, and I thought I wanted a bitch like her. I hated a motherfucker to take from me.

I sent a text message to my dog breeder, letting her know the dogs I had were on the way. I, on the other hand, was headed to see these twin bitches. Not only did they take my dog, but the two look-alike motherfuckers took my money. How she was able to do that credit card trick on me, I don't know.

This here had to be the work of Chance. She and Lyric used to do that card trick shit back in the day. It was time she showed me how she got me outta my money like that.

I called my runner back. "Send a car to that address. Check things out on that end. I'm on my way to y'all as soon as I touch down!" I barked, then I shot a text out to my boy, who owned a jet, after I disconnected my call.

Me: Yo, I need a favor from you.

Within seconds, my phone rang.

Chapter Three

Chance Smith

  To say Lyric had my sister fucked up was an understatement. This bitch had been coming for Chime since she first locked eyes with her. At first, I thought picking with my sister was her way of bonding when she and I were friends. I didn't understand her problem, but I noticed she had one. It was harmless when it started, but then things got real. It was like Lyric was low-key jealous of my sister. She had every right to be. My sister was bad as fuck. Chime just showed it differently.

  We were born identical, but we looked nothing alike. There was a time when no one could tell us apart. We dressed in matching colors, hair and all. My mother wouldn't have it any other way. It was a must that we dressed alike while we were out. I was cool with it, but as the years passed, my sister and I wanted our own style.

  We were close until middle school until Lyric and I became friends. My sister and I fell apart, and I felt bad she didn't hang out with me. It wasn't like I didn't ask her. She just always said no. She told me my crew was too wild for her. I laughed it off, because she was right. It was lit with us.

  I was the life of the party. Bitches knew and loved me to the point where they had to be down with us. I hated having such a cool-ass personality, when my sister didn't. She was like somebody's old ass aunty when it came to her ways. She wore baggy clothes and nothing that showed off her body.

  I couldn't wait until Chime started wearing makeup like she

did for her clients. The girl had a gift with her hands and helped everyone but herself. My sister could turn an ugly bitch into a bad one. She was good with makeup and clothes. She just didn't apply that skill to her own life. However, all that was about to get better for her. She could open her makeup shop with the money I got from Prince's card.

I risked my life and my family's lives by taking Prince's money, but I couldn't help it. It gave me a rush. I put my new dog back in its taxi. I thought I was done with this life, but Lyric and her boyfriend triggered me. I'd been given that life a rest but taking a jab at people looking down at my sister had me back at it again.

I could see if we didn't need the money, but we did. Prince had it, so I stepped out on faith to see if he had it for us. I was glad I did because we needed every penny. My sisters and I have been busting our asses to make ends meet, and we still didn't have enough. Taking this money wasn't okay. I wasn't trying to make excuses for my actions.

If it came down to it, I would go down for my actions. That's why I wouldn't say a word to my older sister. She would turn my ass over to the cops if I left it up to her. At twenty-five, Cinnamon wasn't your ordinary girl. My boo was off the fucking chain. I didn't know who would marry her, but good luck to them.

Cinnamon was and had always been a control freak. Everything had to go her way or no way at all. She would lose sleep just to be in control and right. That was the least of her problems. She was also uptight and low-key. Cinnamon thought she was better than everyone. My mom and grandma praised her until she got pregnant out of wedlock. Her ass got caught slipping, which humbled her for a little while. Her having my niece changed her so much.

I smiled at my new best friend, who was evidence of my spontaneous side. "Well, hello, there, cutie. You're so cute." I cooed over my new pet.

I didn't care if Lyric and her lackeys got another dog, I had to have this one. He was crying and shaking from wearing this hot-ass coat vest. Lyric was swinging the taxi around, not caring that this little cutie was in there. I couldn't stand to see animals being mistreated. If I could make a difference, I would. So, I guess you could say I did. I was in love from the time I heard it cry. We connected eyes, and I had to have it. I waited for them to check in and deleted them from the system. I instructed my coworker to take a break, and I changed the paperwork and made it look like they were never there.

As soon as I opened the pet taxi, the dog jumped right into my arms. She was all over the place, jumping around and giving me kisses. I took the ugly vest it was wearing, with like seven pockets on it, off. I took it and tossed it to the side. Something fell out, but I didn't try to get it. I was so tickled and enjoying this moment that I left everything in the middle of the floor. I played with my new dog in the middle of my room. She was having a ball. I started to think of a name for her.

I wanted to say this was a red-nosed pitbull. This one was a girl, and my niece would love it. My sister would be mad for a while, but she would get over it. She hated it when I did anything for my niece. I would be out and about, see something I wanted her to have, and get it for her. I loved to see my niece smile.

No matter what it was, I got it for London. I didn't have any kids, but I wanted a few. I wanted my daughter to be just as sweet and kind as my niece. She was the only baby in the house, so I spoiled her rotten, and this dog would take the cake.

∞∞∞

It took no time for my new baby to adjust to my house. I let her run around and make herself at home. After a few hours of running, I bathed her, dried her up, and fed her. I then let her play as I cleaned up my house. Once Cinnamon came in and saw the dog, she would flip, so I finished cleaning to butter the situation up a little. Done with the living room and kitchen, all I had left was my room. I would wait until later to do that. A bitch was beaten.

I flopped down on the sofa, putting my feet up. It had already been a long week, and I was glad to see it was over. I pulled my phone out of my bra and went on Facebook. I kept seeing pictures of my sister being shared, making me log right back off. It had been days ago, and people were still joking about it. Lyric had gone too far this time, but it didn't matter. We won in the end. We got off with $250,000 to split, plus the dog.

I might even move out, not too far away from my sisters, though, because I would miss London. I could try to convince my sisters to move, but they didn't want to give up our grandmother's house. Moving was just what we needed to do. We could use a fresh start in a new area. Hell, I was down for moving out of the state. I laid back, thinking hard about life as my sister came through the door.

I jumped to my feet and tried to dash to my room, but I ended up bumping right into Cinnamon. It was a no-go. My sister stood in front of me, blocking my way. "So why are you running, bitch?"

I crossed my arms over one another. "The question is, why are you home so early, hoe?" I snapped back. It was bad enough I had to deal with one sister all the time, but this one was too much.

"Momma, you see the dog," my niece called out, waking up from her sleep. For her to be just four, she was smart as ever. She pointed at the pet taxi next to the door.

I closed my eyes, sat next to London, and waited for it.

"Yes, honey, I do see the doggy, but why do I see a doggy, Chance Amirah Smith?" She called a bitch's full government.

I said nothing, just opened my eyes, and smiled. Out of nowhere, the dog came running and playing with the weird coat vest thingy I threw in the corner earlier. My niece had let the dog out. The smile on her face cleared up anything I was feeling. I did it for this moment alone.

"Somebody gave it to us," I lied to my sister.

"Come better, Pooh. I'm not dumb or slow," Cinnamon snapped.

By the time I opened my mouth, the dog was tugging at the vest, which ripped open. All these white packages of shit dropped out everywhere. I fucked around and panicked when I saw what it was. I raced over to pick up the packages off the floor before my niece or the dog got a hold of them.

After I picked up the last package, I held it up to the light. Knowing just what it was, I shook my head. This nigga used these pets to get drugs on the airplane.

"Somebody gave you a fucking dog, Chance? Huh? You lying-ass little girl. And don't act like I don't know what the fuck that is," Cinnamon continued, ranting.

"Now is not the time. I have to get them out of here." I started to go to my room about the same time Chime came out of her room.

"Tell her about the money you gave me," Chime called out.

It took everything in me not to beat her the fuck up. She knew motherfucking well I was trying to keep that part from Cinnamon.

"Money? Tell me you're not doing the card trick again. Sis, you almost got yourself killed the last time, remember?"

I rolled my eyes. Earlier, I was a bitch. Now, I was her sis.

"What is so hard about working for what you need?"

Cinnamon asked.

What I did had nothing to do with me working. I had a good-paying job, so it was much deeper than that. I could admit that it was more of a come-up for me and payback for Lyric, but I was just not about to do that right now.

"Look, let me figure this out, okay?" I headed to my room.

My so-called twin stood there as I passed by, and I didn't look her way. I wanted so badly to say something, but this was my fault. I couldn't blame her. She was already going through enough. What I knew was we needed to get the fuck out of here. I ran back to my room door and yelled out, "Pack y'all things. We have to go!"

I went into my bathroom, grabbed everything I needed, and stuffed it in my overnight bag. It hit me that no one responded when I told them to pack. I hoped they were listening. This shit just got real. Prince would come for my ass.

I may have been gone twenty minutes, ensuring I had all I needed when I returned to the living room. It was black as hell, like the light was cut off. I could hear something, but I didn't see a thing.

"Who cut the lights off and wants to be playing at a time like this?"

All hell broke loose as soon as I cut the light switch on. My sisters and niece were seated in a row, tied to a chair.

"Oh my God! What's going on?" I asked. As the words left my lips, I was pushed to the floor.

"Glad you could join us." Prince said with his gun aimed directly at my head. His crew had their guns aimed at my sister and niece. If I felt bad for anyone, it was my niece who was crying full tears.

I almost shitted my pants seeing masked men in my house. Once I hit the floor, they picked me up and placed me in a chair, but not without a fight. I was working big boy's ass. I didn't want to overdo shit and get us killed, so I gave in.

"What do you want, and why are you here?" Cinnamon asked as she tried to reach my niece. It was useless. We were tied down too tight.

"So, which one of you Doublemint twins stole my dog and dope?" Prince grilled.

The entire room was silent. Both my sisters looked my way, just like a snitch. On the other hand, I had my eyes on them, trying to see my way out if I had one. I wasn't coming off the dog, but he could have the dope. I told myself to play like I was hard, because Prince didn't mention the money. Maybe he didn't know about the money.

"So, I'ma ask one more time, even though I know who got me. Start talking, or we gon' start shooting in this bitch. Until I get answers straight out of the thief's mouth, I'm taking little mama with me." Prince pointed to my niece.

Cinnamon lost her nuts. She wiggled around, screaming and kicking, trying to get to Prince.

"I took the dog and dope. Take me," Chime lied.

Before I could respond, Prince hit her with the end of his gun, knocking her chair to the floor. He then cut the ropes off her, picked her up, and left us all sitting there crying. Cinnamon looked at me with so much hurt and pain in her eyes. I knew what she was thinking and wanted it to be me, too.

I looked from my sister to my niece and broke down. I raced to the door to see if they were still outside. It was no use. They were already gone in the wind. I should have spoken up for Chime. Now, I didn't know if she would live or die. I untied my niece and sister.

One thing I knew was my sister talked to us about always

having our location on. I hoped to God this was one of those moments Chime listened. I went straight to my phone and pulled up Chime's location. She wasn't even ten minutes away. I jumped up and dashed to my room, grabbing my keys.

"Wait, are you leaving us here alone?" Cinnamon asked. She didn't want to be alone after what she saw.

"I pulled up Chime's location. I'm going to get my sister." I explained as I walked over to my hall closet and pulled down a Jordan box from the back. I held the box close to me and placed it on the table. Once I safely had it on the table, I pulled out the gun and stuck it in my back pants.

"What are you going to do with that, Chance? Do you even know how to use that thing?" Cinnamon asked. At this point, she was plucking my nerves. She picked the wrong time to be nagging.

Hearing her mouth only made me go harder. What my sister didn't know was that I'd had this gun for a while. I only had to use it once since I got it, and today would make twice if things went wrong. I gathered everything I needed, because I wasn't returning to this house until Chime was with me. Whatever Prince was on, I was on it too.

"Well, I'm coming with you. Let's drop London off at her sitter." Cinnamon grabbed London and her bag and chased behind me.

Chapter Four

Lyric Dior

Fuck I look like becoming second to any bitch? I don't care if it's his mother, sister, or child, none of that shit rocks with a bitch like me. I was stingy, even when it came down to having kids — nope. I wasn't taking care of shit. I needed my man and his time all to myself. That's part of the reason I had to lie to Prince about losing my baby. That wasn't the case at all. A bitch just didn't know who the father of my daughter, Harmony was.

I paid my godmother to raise Harmony. She knew the real me and knew taking care of a child wouldn't fit my life. I knew I'd be a bad mother, but I didn't care. My godmother lived nine hours away, so Prince would never bump into her. I came over here every so often to check on her. She always gave me the *I'm not going to be here long* talk and told me how I needed to get my shit in order.

The problem was that my godmother was getting old. I couldn't handle the thought of losing her. What would I do if I lost her? Who would I have to fall back on? She was the only family I had. I didn't tell Prince about her 'cause I stashed my daughter with her. I was there to check in but had to be back by morning, which meant I was only staying a few hours. Shit, that was how much time I could spend with the little girl before she got on my nerves.

Her little ass was a pain in the butt, and she had the nerve to talk back. My godmother let her get away with anything. I guess it was because she was old now. I walked in using my key and headed straight for the living room.

"Well, if it isn't my deadbeat ass mother!" My daughter yelled.

All I could do was shake my head and walk right past her. I didn't so much as give her a hug or even speak. The child hated me, so I left it at that.

I dropped down on the day sofa and kicked my feet up. I looked over at Harmony and smiled, because she looked just like me, had my attitude, and all her little ass knew was how to be mad. I guessed she felt me looking at her 'cause she flicked me off. Her badass pointed her middle finger right at me like I wasn't her mother or even gave a fuck that I was. I couldn't blame her. I never did anything for her.

"What I tell you about smart-talking your mother, Harmony?" Grams asked. Although she is my godmother, her nickname has always been Grams, which makes her more endearing to me. She pushed her wheelchair into the living room.

My daughter got up and helped her take her spot next to the day chair. I didn't get up to help, because I just drove nine hours and was exhausted from my trip. I needed a nap and some food to do it all over again.

"You told me don't let you see me do it, Grams. That's what you told me, and I didn't see you coming this way, so I'm sorry."

I ignored Harmony's badass, closed my eyes, and tried to sleep. Knowing them, that wouldn't happen. Grams missed me like crazy and wished she could help me get my priorities right, but I was too far gone and careless. Grams was going blind, so she couldn't tell what I looked like lately.

"Tell her about the man who came here looking for her." Harmony said, causing me to sit straight up.

"What man? When did he come? What did he say?" I asked, scared as hell. Who could be looking for me and here of all places?

"He said he's Harmony's dad and left her a lot of money. He

also gave a letter to her to give to you."

I got up so fast. I knew who it was, and I hated knowing he was back. Slime was out to get me, but I wouldn't let him. That man was madly in love with me, but I broke things off. He'd been blackmailing me for years, and I was free from it when he and his dad got locked up. I got back right with Prince, and things were good until now.

"I have to go. Love y'all." Was all I said as I left out the door, flying. I didn't leave the money I had for them or anything. I just took off.

Once I hit my car, I jumped in and started the engine. I pulled off fast as hell, only to be met by the devil himself in my back seat.

"Why are you so in a rush, ma? I just got back. Pullover right here so you can suck on this dick right fast." Slime instructed, pointing his gun at my head.

My heart dropped to my feet, but I did as I was told. I parked the car, and he got out of the back and came to the driver's side, still pointing the gun at me. He opened the door, and I slid over to the passenger seat while he got inside.

"So, how are you and my little girl doing? Or do you know 'cause you ain't been there to see her in a while? Anyway, does my cousin know we got a daughter?" He asked as he pulled his dick out with one hand and motioned for me to serve him before he pulled off. "We gone have to tell him soon if you don't move quicker than that." Slime threatened when I hesitated.

I went in for the kill and sucked the hell out of his little ass dick. I treated that dick like it was the biggest dick I had ever sucked. "I missed you, daddy," I lied, making this shit worthwhile.

All he did was shoot cum in my mouth, which jetted down my throat. He moaned like a bitch as he drove wildly on the highway. I started to sit up, and he knocked the hell out of me. I went fast to sleep.

∞∞∞

Hours later, we stood in front of Prince's gate hand in hand.

"Why are you doing this to me? I told you he doesn't know I have a child." I was about to have a heart attack. The last thing I needed was for Prince to come out of the house and see me standing there with Slime.

"Because you played me this entire time, knowing you would never be with a nigga. Bitch, you were just stringing me along." Slime hit me twice in the face and pulled me to the front door by the back of my hair.

"No, baby, you have it all wrong. I never loved him. It's always been you and me. We have a family now." I tried to butter his big ass up. He was a sucker for love. I guess he lacked the shit coming up.

Slime and I had a lot in common when we started messing around. We both were well-hated and always got overlooked. We played in the background until our time came. I was wrong for playing with his feelings. I think I got myself in too deep with this one. Slime was bat shit crazy, but nothing and no one had Prince beat when it came to crazy. It was sad that Slime hated Prince, because he couldn't be him.

I had to listen to how he hated coming up second to Prince. Slime would go on for hours about how his dad and uncle praised him. Hell, to me, the hate he had for Prince only made him a fan. Slime wanted to be Prince for all the wrong reasons. It had nothing to do with the accomplishments he had under his belt. He wanted Prince out of the way for good. I hated that I was responsible for putting him in jail the first time.

Prince got locked up because I wanted Slime to take his place in the game for a while, so I set Prince up. I called the narcotic hotline and told them Prince had guns and dope in the car. I sent my location and waited for them to come. I made sure he had his gun on him. As for the dope, I ended up changing my mind and stashing it. I didn't need him locked away for life, just long enough for me to hide Slime and my daughter.

The day Prince got pulled over, he knew something was off. He kept telling me something didn't feel right about that day. That man was always right when he had a gut feeling. It was me telling him to ignore it. I felt terrible at first, but then I found out about his money. I needed parts of getting that bread. It wasn't like he didn't take care of me because he did. I just wanted more than what he was offering me. I wanted half of everything to where you would think I had that man's last name. I wanted the house, restaurants, car shops, and everything I could get my hands on. I got the shocker of my life when Prince's two brothers came and took over.

It became harder to put Slime in his place. After Prince was sentenced, I had to think of a way for him to keep me around. Of course, the number one trick in the game was a baby. I told him I was pregnant and didn't get pregnant until after I told him. He was locked up when I found out, so I knew my daughter didn't belong to Prince. It broke my heart for a while, having to lie to him, knowing how much he wanted a family. I wasn't sure if I'd ever tell him I hated kids and didn't want them. It just felt safer keeping that part to myself.

I kissed Slime's lips and face to bring him back to my level. As I said before, he was a sucker for love and affection. I put my hands in his sweatpants and played with the little guy between his legs. I pulled him back into the car within seconds, getting him away from the two cameras Prince had just put up. It would be just my luck if he pulled up while I was doing this. There was no doubt in my mind that he would kill us both.

"Where are you staying now?" Slime asked, making my heart

skip a beat. He had fallen for my bullshit again.

Once we got in the car, I pulled off. We were going to my place in the country. One thing Prince and I never did was move in together. He made it clear he wanted his space, and I agreed because I needed mine. I didn't so much as spend the night at his house. He didn't play that. When we spent time together, we went to one of the three vacation homes he had a few hours away, or Prince would stay at the condo he put me in and paid for. Come to think of it, we never really talked about the future or being a couple. I guessed Prince wanted me out of the picture once he got out of prison.

I drove in silence the whole way there, unsure of what to do next. Thinking about being called out by those two twin bitches on the flight to New York embarrassed me again. It was one thing for Chance to come at me, but not her sister, too. Chime knew she had my ass to kiss.

I disliked Chime with everything in me. The girl had done nothing wrong to me, but I hated her. She was too perfect back in school, and I saw how Prince lusted over her. I just never knew what he saw in her. If basic was a person, she would win the category. For her to be so good with hair and makeup, there was no way she didn't apply that to herself. So, I thought picking on her would make the bitch boss up.

She didn't have to do much because she had it all — hair, looks, body, and even eyes. Deep down, I may have been secretly in love with her the way I obsessed over her. Posting her on Facebook was just a warning. She and I both knew Prince was interested in her. Why? Probably for the same reasons I hated her. He was gentle and kind whenever he got around her. Chime may be able to bring something better than I could out of him.

"Bitch, you over there thinking about that pussy nigga?" Slime yelled.

I almost wanted to tell his ass, yes, but I wanted to make it home safe. "No, baby, I'm thinking about how I'm about to attack that dick," my lying ass told him.

That was all he needed to hear to sit the fuck back and ride. I didn't know how or when, but I had to kill this man, and that had to be soon before he killed me.

Chapter Five

Chime

I woke up in a puddle of blood. The last thing I remembered was admitting to something I didn't do. Then, boom, I was hit over the head. I tried to wipe the blood from my eyes to see. I needed to make out where I was to plan my exit. One thing about me, I was a fighter, so going out without a fight was out of the question. I wanted to scream out, but it wouldn't do any good. I didn't want them to know I was up. Prince was already pissed that his things were stolen from him. I, too, wouldn't have any conversation, let alone sympathy for someone that stole from me.

I sat up off the cold steel floors and leaned against a brick wall. It was cold as hell. I was in somebody's old ass basement. It was dark and stuffy, but a door was on the other side of the room. I couldn't say how long I'd been out, but it had been a few hours. I could barely move, and my eye was damn near glued shut. I couldn't believe Prince hit me like that. He had that killer shit in him, but I didn't know he would show that side of himself to me.

The sound of keys and footsteps from the hall snapped me out of my thoughts. I didn't know if I wanted to run for it or see what he was about to do with me. He didn't try to kill me, or I would be dead by now. I figured I was being held hostage until he got back his dope and dog.

I laid back down on the floor, playing like I was still out cold. I heard the key unlock the door and footsteps coming toward me. I felt somebody walking up to me.

"I know you up. We've been watching you on camera."

I didn't know if I should sit up or still play dead. Either way, Prince had my ass, so it didn't matter. I would make this shit easy for myself. The man had already tied my entire family up and knocked my ass out. I sat up and opened my eyes.

He snapped a finger, and the lights came on.

I could have snapped my fingers minutes ago if that were all I had to do to see in this bitch. I struggled to open my swollen eyes. Prince did a number on me, but I wouldn't say anything.

"Stand up and follow me!" He roared, his voice traveling throughout the basement with an echo. He was mad and ready to kill my ass. That alone made me jump up and do as he said.

I followed Prince out of the basement and into the hallway. We walked up some stairs and from what I could tell, we were in a big ass house. He took me through a side door and outside. As soon as I felt the outside air, I was about to run for it, but I didn't know where I was, and he would shoot my ass.

As we walked to the side of the house, I noticed all the cameras moving with us as we walked. We made a right, and it took us to a path that led to another house. This house was too beautiful, all white with a front water view. With the vision in one eye still good, I could still see everything I needed in case I needed to get out and fast. Prince took us through a backyard with a keypad lock on a fence. He used a keycard hanging from his neck, which opened the gate.

As soon as we reached a glass box, he motioned for me to step into it. I hesitated for a minute, but I did as he asked. Once I stepped in, a machine voice came on and welcomed Prince. He gave it an order, and it started talking immediately. As I was standing in the glass box, it made a funny noise. The computer device scanned my body. As it passed my eyes and ears, it began talking to Prince. It sounded like the computer was reading him my clothes size, hair color, eyes, and all.

Once the scanning was done, the machine sprayed me down with something. Then, it told me to place my hands on the handprints before me. I followed directions and did just that. It flashed light like it took my prints. Within a second, I looked at the screen and saw pictures of myself from years ago with my grandma and mother. It had baby pictures when I was dressed like my sister. It was amazing. Our names, middle names, and nicknames came up. This was some FBI shit. Why did he have all this? He was doing a background check right in front of me.

"Take your clothes off," he ordered once the scan was done.

Prince asking me to undress was too much for me. I became overwhelmed and stumbled. He rushed over, grabbed me, and helped me to my feet. He picked me up and carried me into the house, down the hall, and into the master bedroom. I was light-headed, so I didn't fight him. He placed me on the bed and went to the bathroom. I could hear water running as I lay back. I couldn't see him, but I could feel his presence.

"My worker will get the things you need to handle your hygiene. Take a bath and get right. Then join me so we can start this new job," Prince instructed.

I forced myself off the bed and into the bathroom. I was fucked up physically, mentally, and emotionally. I'd never in my life been in this type of situation. I pulled off all my clothes as I tested the water. The maid came in and left a towel, washrag, clothes, peroxide, soap and some bandages by the sink. I grabbed the cloth, Dove body wash, and peroxide.

As soon as my body touched the water, it relaxed. It took a toll off me just to be able to wash my ass. I felt dirty and flat-out ugly. I wouldn't even look in the mirror when I was naked. I hated who I was.

I laid back fully in the bathtub. After thoroughly wetting my hair, I carefully washed my face, ears, and eyes. Once I was done washing everything twice, I cleaned my swollen eye. It took all of thirty minutes to finish cleaning my body and hair.

As I dried off, I slid on the slippers left for me. I could see much better, making me want to look in the mirror. I wiped the mirror clear of fog and stared at myself. My hair was all over the place, and I didn't care. My eye didn't look too bad. It would take a week to completely heal. That's if I didn't piss Prince off and get beaten again. I was thankful he didn't let me fall earlier. He could have been an ass and let me hit the floor since he thought I stole from him. I felt bad 'cause now I was under his command. It was no telling what he would have me do.

I put on the clothes the lady left me and just let my hair hang. Waiting on the edge of the bed for Prince to come back for me, it was clear he wanted me to work for him, which was fine as long as my family and I were alive. I wanted to talk to them just to let them know I was okay. They had to be worried, probably thinking I was dead. I needed to see if he'd let me use his phone since he took mine.

I shook my head to fight back my tears. I didn't belong here, and Prince knew I wasn't this person. I missed my family and needed to know how they were. Hell, I needed to be with them and wanted to go home.

"You ready? Follow me," Prince's voice broke me from my thoughts. He looked mean, with every vein in his neck popping out.

I couldn't believe how sexy he still was. Even though I was about to die, I was still crushing on him. I didn't know if it was the way his voice echoed or if his presence alone made me feel weird. I figured it was now or never if I wanted to ask about my family. Now was the time for me to speak up.

"If you don't mind, I'd like to use the phone to let my family know I'm fine. Also, you don't need to yell at me. I'm not a child. I can hear you just fine, and these clothes are way too small."

Prince looked at me and laughed like I said something funny.

I crossed my arms and shook my head. I couldn't work under these conditions. He would have to do better. I kept from making eye-to-eye contact with him, waiting on his response, which better had been more than a laugh. I started twiddling my fingers. At this point, it was like we were back in high school and talking for the first time. I got this feeling he wasn't going to hurt me anymore than he already had.

"Damn, ma, so kidnapping you came with a to-do list? Oh, and the clothes fit you just right. You need to take notes. You look decent. You and Queen are the same size, so she looked out for you. I had you measured when you walked in, remember? I know I didn't hit you that hard. Anyway, you're funny, cute, but funny. Now come on before I yell at your sensitive ass for real."

He sped up, walking us into a big room with a computer and some credit card scanners. There had to be over fifty different credit card machines. Prince motioned for me to sit at the table with the machines.

"I want you to do that credit card trick to every customer I send you. Each one will come with paperwork as you swipe the card. Take out one hundred thousand from each."

Confused, I walked over slowly and took a seat. I took the scene in and was scared. It wasn't that I didn't know how to do it. I had taught my sister everything she knew. The problem was not getting murdered by the people whose money I was about to help Prince steal.

"How long do I have to do this? And what about my request?" I asked.

"Look, ma, this is not a radio station. I ain't taking requests. You will leave when I'm done with you." Prince smiled hard at that last statement, which had me ready to walk out. His smile let me know he had me in this for life.

He handed me a code to put on the computer. I punched in the code, and it pulled up a crazy screen. He then typed a code in, and it went to windows. He went over everything he needed me to do, which was easy. I knew the software already, so it took no time to start. The customers started rolling in, and he sat next to me, leaving a gun on the table for me to see. His brothers came in and set up shop.

∞∞∞

I had been here for hours and was ready to go. Then, King placed a laptop in front of me. I paid it no mind because he had me fucked up if he thought I was working for him, too. He then put another machine next to the computer he was using. He powered it up, and it came right on. I'd be damned if it didn't look like the one from work.

Once the system fully booted up, it blew my mind. It was just like the one from work with more quality. Somehow, they had my information to get into the airport system at work. I wondered what they were about to have me doing now. The same way we hit them was how they wanted me to get others.

"Oh, you pretty as fuck with all that good, long hair you got. We'll have some cute ass babies fucking with me," a heavy-set guy flirted, making my skin itch. He had the nerve to wear a Nike outfit that was too small. He was wearing it like a belly shirt at this point.

"She ain't here for all that, nigga. You flying somewhere or what?" Prince chimed in like he was saving a bitch or something.

I completely ignored the attempt to protect me.

"Put your information in the airport data, ma," Prince ordered.

I entered my information. Prince pressed a key, and an entirely new airline opened. He turned the keyboard to where I couldn't see it and typed fast. After he was done, he tapped me.

"You can book these flights, too. Just use this key, tap it once, and type in where he's going. Choose an airport, charge him, and print the shit out. Got it?" Prince didn't wait for my response. He took the big dude to the side and sent him out of the room.

I hit each card for the amount I was told, plus the fee to fly for the next twenty people.

∞∞∞

I had been at it for a good eight hours straight with no bathroom breaks or food. I was dead tired and ready to go. They had more than enough money just off today alone, so I should be taken home. We should be free.

"I need to use the bathroom," I told Prince.

He glanced at the clock, looking shocked it was late. "My bad. You're way past your work hours. I ain't paying you extra either."

Everyone in the room laughed but me. Prince wasn't funny at all. He tried too hard. I waited for them to stop laughing, because I had to use the bathroom. I stood up and waited for him to lead the way.

"I'ma take our guest to her room and get her to settle. Y'all niggas meet me in the man cave." Prince told his crew as he walked me out of the room and into the hallway.

When we returned to the master bedroom, I took off for the bathroom. Prince closed the room door before I could react. I ignored him and used the bathroom.

"Hurry and do what you need. I'll be waiting." Prince ordered on the other side of the bathroom door.

This was the first time all day that I relieved myself, and he was rushing me. I cried as soon as I was done using the toilet. This was a failure. Why did I have such a fucked-up life? Why didn't God like my family and me? The more I thought about these last twenty-four hours, the harder the tears fell.

Prince walked in, and I didn't even care. He saw me at my lowest. I was this low because of him and his girlfriend. This was their fault for being such assholes. Chance would have never taken his money and dog if Lyric weren't acting like a bitch at the airport.

"You wanna fight?" his rude ass asked.

I jumped up, raced to him, and started swinging on his ass. One hit after another connected to his face and head. He wasn't trying to hurt me 'cause all he did was yank me up and walk me to the bed. The next thing I knew, I was slammed against the bed with both arms over my head. His body was on top of mine as we breathed hard as hell. I couldn't say a word as we tried to catch our breaths at the same time. That's when he leaned in and kissed me.

Once Prince let my arms go, I pulled his body close to mine and started for his jeans. I didn't know what I was doing. I'd never had sex before, but he turned me on in a sick, crazy way. As we kissed, he slipped his tongue into my mouth. I returned the same pleasure he was giving me. Once I reached his dick, my breathing got harder. He was a good ten inches thick. I started to pull it out, but he stopped me.

"You're not ready for this dick, ma. Get you some rest, and I'ma send your phone in here." He got up and fixed his clothes before leaving the room.

As promised, seconds later, Prince returned with my cell phone.

I called my sisters on three-way, assuring them I was good,

HONOR THY SAVAGE

and that Prince and I were working as a team. We talked for hours, and I was glad they stopped worrying about me. I would ask Prince to take me to spend this coming weekend with them.

Chapter Six

Prince

I had to stop myself from giving her this dick. Shawty wasn't ready for a nigga like me. I wasn't sure what came over me that made me kiss her. Her smart mouth was hell, which had my dick hard as a rock. It turned me on when a bitch had a quick tongue.

After I pulled away from our kiss, I came back to earth. I knew better than to go this far with Chime. I couldn't help it. Even though she was here for the wrong reasons, I didn't need to be sidetracked. It almost felt like we were back in our high school days for a second. I felt bad for hitting her with the gun, but I needed to knock Chime out so she wouldn't see where I was taking her. I even considered blindfolding her, but I wasn't sure if she'd put up a fight.

Walking into my man cave, I was glad my brothers stuck around. We needed to get down to business right away. Knowing them, they had some shit to say. I could tell by the way they watched me with Chime. These niggas knew me better than I knew myself, so I waited for it.

"Did you move the girl into your house? Damn, her ass got a little pull, doesn't she?" Major joked.

I see these niggas started early on joke time. I didn't have a laugh or a smile for them. They had me fucked up right now. We had real shit to handle, but they had jokes. I wasn't sure why I was so triggered. What they were saying had some truth to it. She would never have made it if it had not been for who she was. Chime would have been dead, but something told me it wasn't her doing it. She wasn't even around when my payment got processed. It was her sister that took both the dog and my money. Still, Chime standing up for her sister and family said a lot.

"So that's bae?" King laughed as he and Major dapped each other up. They went on about this Chime shit for the next twenty minutes.

When my guest arrived, they acted like killers as soon as the motion detector went off. They reached for their guns at the same time. Finally, these niggas remembered they were killers and not comedians.

"Ain't no need to get on game time now," I said and proceeded to open the door for my company. I had my on-call crew come through so we could resolve an issue.

When going over my weekly check-in with the videos I had set up, I put my foot in my mouth and said niggas wouldn't try me. However, last night my runner was hit for some of the work.

"Welcome, gentlemen. As you all know, we are here for one reason and one reason only: to find my money and product. Today would have been payday for you niggas, but truthfully, ion think you motherfuckers deserve your money until you get mine back." I announced as everyone came in and took a seat.

The entire room knew what I was on by now. I wasn't the type of nigga to beat around the bush. I didn't do business like that. I was straightforward. The only thing I was trying to get to the bottom of was my money. The room got quiet, making me wonder what everyone else was here for. I wanted to know how this even came about. There was no way I was in a room full of goons, yet I could hear a pencil drop.

"I called you all here for a reason, and it was to get my shit back," I reminded them.

These motherfuckers had the nerve to look around like they knew nothing about it. I reached for my gun and sat the shit on the table before them.

"So, I'ma say this again. Maybe y'all didn't hear me. What happened to my fucking dope?" They had three seconds to respond, or I was killing them all.

Niggas found a voice all at the same time.

"Boss, I don't remember for real. All I remember was being hit over the head as I opened my car door. I saw the nigga who hit me, and you won't believe who it was," Dexx said. "I would have told you sooner, but I couldn't place his name until the other morning."

My trigger finger went shaking. I didn't believe Dexx didn't know his name until now. None of that shit sounded right to me. This shit was starting to be too good to be true. I let everyone leave the room but Dexx. There was no need for this information to get out to everyone. It was for my brothers and me at this point. One thing about me was that I was far from being messy. My beef was just that.

I stood over Dexx with my hands crossed, trying to read him. He looked nervous. I saw that from the jump. I waited for him to speak to see where his mind was.

"So, you know who hit you? Go head talk, nigga. I'm listening," Major came out and asked after waiting for one of us to speak up.

Dexx started to talk, but I stopped him because I got a text. The text told me that my hidden camera got a clear shot of the person who hit him. This was perfect timing, I would say. I wanted to see if Dexx's story was about to add up. I went ahead and connected my phone to the computer in front of us, typed in my code, and played the video.

Dexx lied about what happened to him. He looked comfortable talking to whoever was on the other side. I couldn't make out who he was talking to, because the person stayed away from the camera. It looked to me that Dexx was telling him to stay that far from it. I used the code my IT told me to use and zoomed in on it. I froze the camera and zoomed in on the face, which gave me a different angle. It was clear as day who Dexx was talking to, and he knew damn well this nigga wasn't welcome anywhere around my property.

"Look, man, it's not what it looks like. That nigga came to me at my house while I was sleeping. He wasn't by himself. A motherfucker you are close to came with him. They told me they needed in on that drop your boy told him about, or he would kill my twin brother and kids!" Dexx spat out.

I didn't want to sound cold-hearted, but he knew what the fuck he signed up for when it came to our business. One thing about it, had he come to me and told me about that nigga I would have done something. In my eyes, he betrayed me by siding with this nigga and whoever else he was with. He helped him set me up to get robbed. He knew I would go hard for his family like it was my own. Dexx should have come to me, so now I have to handle him.

"You didn't trust me enough to tell me he came for your family? How long have I been caring for you and your family?" I slid on my gloves.

Dexx jumped up and started begging for his life. The problem was he was more scared of what that nigga would do to him than me. That wasn't how things worked around here.

"Look, I can bring him to you. Please don't do this. I have a family that needs me," he cried.

I smiled 'cause he was willing to give up the nigga's whereabouts now, which was cool. That information was vital to me as well. I reached into the desk and pulled out a pen and some paper. "Write all that down and let's go," I ordered.

Dexx looked at me with hurt in his eyes. He knew this was

the last time he would see his family. I did plan to make him keep his word to reel my uncle and little cousin in for me.

"So, you saw my Uncle Peanut beforehand, and made a deal with him but said nothing?" Major asked, walking up on Dexx.

Dexx didn't even look my brother in the eyes. He remained with his head down, only further pissing my brother off. I was more patient than King and Major. They had absolutely no chill. They were ready to kill Dexx right there and then.

I spoke up just to clear the air. "We need him, so let's go, Dexx. Call him and tell him to meet you, because I have another drop for him tomorrow."

He pulled out his phone and started his text. He let me read what he wrote, and I okayed it for him to send. While we waited for a response, I made other arrangements. He wanted a drop, so I gave him one he would never forget. Besides, my uncle and I had unfinished business. I shouldn't have saved my uncle the first time my brothers wanted him dead. He was bad blood in the family, and I didn't need anybody with that type of hate in my family alive.

I set up a time and day to meet with some weight for my uncle. That would give me a few days to see what my numbers are coming in like. It's only been a few days, but my shop was booming. I made my way back to my spot, making sure Dexx knew the deal. Of course, I had my men on him, so it wasn't like he was being let off easy.

It took a few days, but all plans were set. Lexx was happy to hear from me. I let him know what I had going on so it wouldn't catch anyone off guard. He gave me the okay, and it was a done deal.

∞∞∞

I sent for Dexx, and hours later, he showed up unwillingly. I made him send out a text to my Uncle Peanut. I told him to let him know the drop was ready on his end. Dexx received a text message saying to meet him in the same spot, making me even madder 'cause they had been meeting up. I let the nigga respond the way he wanted to. Then, I made him write the address to their meeting spot.

Once I got all I needed, I nodded for my brothers to handle it. Seconds later, I heard a gunshot, and Dexx's body hit the ground shortly after. He had it coming one way or another. I would make sure his family would be straight. They had nothing to do with his switch-up.

I sent a text to my clean-up crew, gathered all I needed from the table, and headed out the back. After saying goodbye to my brother, I went back to the stash house. I was ready to see my uncle's face when he saw me. This was going to happen one way or another.

He'd been out a little while. I just didn't think the nigga would return this way. I got word that Uncle Peanut was back on the streets three weeks ago, but thought he would have left the fucking state. I planned to give it to the nigga the way he'd been asking for it. He and his son both had hearts. That's the only thing we had in common. I would just say my heart was purer.

I needed to clear my mind ASAP. I would be lying had I said I wasn't thinking about shawty. I was still trying to shake off that kiss we shared. I didn't want it to feel that good.

My dick got rock hard out of the blue when I reached Chime's room. Just thinking of her had a nigga gone. It'd been a while since I had these kinds of feelings. I would be lying if I said I didn't miss it. At this point, I was ready to give her something real in her life, but I had too much shit going on. Dealing with Lyric was more than enough.

I couldn't help but question Lyric's loyalty. She lived two different lives. She was hiding something from me, and I planned to find out what. Hell, it had even been said she had everything to do with me going to jail. Niggas said she had a nigga ready to take my spot in the game. No one said who the nigga was she was fucking, though.

I took care of Lyric from the heart. That day I got locked up was crazy, because I didn't have any work on me. How they found that shit in my car was beyond me. Still, the word was she set me up, so I can't help but think this bitch must have stashed my dope in her pussy to pull that off. I struggled to believe she had set me up. I couldn't say I was in love with her, though. I had sex with her and let her give me head, but that was it. Even though the sex was getting old, I was used to her. I had never been the type to fuck around with different bitches.

Hoes didn't excite me. A well-minded woman did. So, the question was how did I end up with Lyric? She wasn't always this off the chain. When she lost her mother, she lost herself. She needed me, so I stood in the gap. I stayed down for her just like she had been there for me. I didn't call that love. It was loyalty.

I knocked on the master bedroom door, knowing damn well, even though I told her she could leave, I really kidnapped Chime. Now, I could see why these niggas were clowning me. I was making a fool out of myself. I didn't wait for her to answer before entering the room, but I'd fucked up by knocking, anyway. I noticed she was fast asleep when I opened the door, so I locked her in the room and headed to my main house.

I needed a hot shower and some loud. This had been a fucked-up ass day, but I was getting to the bottom of my issues. I reached my room and headed for my bathroom. I started my shower and pulled my clothes off. My mind must have been playing tricks on me. Once I closed my eyes, I imagined seeing Chime naked.

My dick rocked up the second Chime's face came to mind. I wanted her badly, but this vision was the best thing I had had in a while. While I took my shower, I thought of her washing her body head to toe without leaving any dry areas. I'd cleaned her face with one rag and used another for her body. The water ran down my back as I jacked my dick off. I needed some pussy and bad, but with how things looked, I'd have to wait.

Once I got that relief, I washed all over again, got out, dried off, and put on my boxers. Dead ass tired, it wouldn't take much for me to go to sleep. I took my stash out of my desk, rolled a fat blunt, and lit the fat end of it as I laid back on my bed. I had an all-black king-size bedroom set, California style. I had a brand-new ass bed but never was in it. I was always on the move.

I needed to close my eyes for a few hours. I'd been up for three days, and that was all my body could take. I hit the blunt and took my mind off my day. Blowing the smoke out like a pro smoker, I finished the blunt and cut the television to ESPN. I didn't know who was playing or what was on. I had to have the television on so I could sleep. It took all of ten minutes for me to pass out.

∞∞∞

Dexx didn't give me the correct address, it was that or Peanut was out there watching me. I felt he may have tipped him off in their last text. I went by that address the day he gave it to me. As I checked out the area, I saw an old lady in a wheelchair and a little girl, but not once did I see who I needed to see.

I think he pulled a fast one on me because he knew he would die. I started my car to leave and thought my eyes were fucking with me. The little girl that came out of that house looked just like Lyric. I had to be tripping. I was nine hours away.

Pulling out of the driveway, I headed to a hotel. I didn't want to drive back home tonight. My brothers followed behind me. As we reached a stop sign, a car ran into the side of my car. My car slid across the road and into a tree. I could hear some words being said but couldn't make out what. The sound of gunshots made me reach for my gun.

Major raced over to me. "Y'all good?"

"I'm good, bruh!" I yelled, trying to get my mind right. I'd just gotten out of my seatbelt and kicked the front window in to get out. After the glass had all fallen, I climbed out the window. By the time I reached the ground, the shootout had stopped.

King pulled up on the side of me. I got in the front seat and sat back, wondering if anybody saw who hit me. I wasn't a fool. I knew who it was but spotting him was what I needed. This shit was now outta hand and for no reason.

Slime and Peanut were behind this. They knew I was coming for them. There were no words that needed to be said when I saw them.

"That was Slime and Peanut. I saw them both with my own eyes. So, what's the move, because these niggas forgot how we got down, I see?" Major asked.

"It's time we jog their memory!" King snapped.

I was on another level right now. Not only did this nigga set me up, but he also just ran me off the road. Slime and Peanut had to pay. I was on some other shit, and this town wouldn't sleep until I got revenge. I sent out a text to my whole crew, putting a price on these niggas' heads that alone would wake everyone up.

After the police came and took my information, I refused to be seen in the emergency room. I got the information about where my car was towed and headed to the hotel room. Once I checked in, I took the time to pull up Lyric's Facebook and went through all her pictures. That's when I saw the older lady in the wheelchair, but she looked much younger. I saved the image with Lyric and the lady and made plans to visit the address Dexx had given me to get some answers out of her.

I laid back, resting my eyes, letting this shit hit me. My phone started going off like crazy. I looked to see who said anything I needed to hear. Glad everyone was on board with this shit, I figured by the end of the day, the whole city would be looking for Slime and Peanut.

My phone rang and seeing that it was Lyric gave me a bad taste in my mouth. I picked up on the second ring. "Yo?" I answered, not in the mood for the shit she had to say.

"Why haven't I seen you in a while?" She sounded like shit was sweet, and she missed a nigga. Little did she know I was truly done with her.

"You know my dog got stolen from me by the twins. Maybe had you not pissed them off, I wouldn't have to clean this mess up. I don't need you around, running off that mouth when I'm talking business." That was all she needed to know. I hung up, not waiting for her to reply. Trying to get her to understand where I was coming from was like pulling teeth. Lyric was only going to see shit her way. In her mind, I was already cheating.

Lyric was right, in a sense. This time, she would hate that it was Chime. I'd been low-key in love with Chime since grade school. I only picked on her 'cause I liked her. That's what kids did back then, but she never paid me any mind. I used to write little letters to her, and my whole class thought she was sending the shit to herself.

I knew everything there was to know about Chime. Her favorite color was purple. Her favorite foods were tacos and pizza. I learned that from watching her bring lunch to school. I noticed everything she did, every mark visible on her body, what made her smile, and the dimple on her right cheek when she graced us with her smile.

∞∞∞

The Next Morning

It fucked me up to find out who that little girl belonged to. After I gave the old lady the rundown of how I got her address and that picture, she told me everything. Slime and Lyric had a baby on me, and it took my soul. I wasn't the emotional type, but a nigga felt like I had been stabbed in the chest. I gave the old lady my contact information, so she could get in touch with me. I still needed a blood test. Lyric was now on my hit list, along with Peanut and Slime.

I was now back home pulling into my driveway. With all a nigga had on the mind, I couldn't help but laugh. I'd been thinking about shawty this entire ride. I needed to be worried about other shit, but Chime was at the top of my mind.

"Good looking out. I'll get at y'all niggas later," I told my brothers as I exited the car.

I hit the gate code as they backed out and left. I set the alarm once I was in and refreshed my cameras. I went into the house and checked on my sister and Chime. Queen was left in charge. She was the only one I trusted with Chime and my money.

My sister was also my bookkeeper, so she knew the job. Chime had two clients, so I didn't bother them. I headed straight for my room to handle my hygiene. After I was done, I sent for Chime. My sister walked in with Chime. One thing about my sister, she could run her mouth. That's why she and Lyric became so tight.

"Hey, big bruh, I got Ms. Chime here for you." She said, smiling so hard that I almost asked her what the fuck was so funny.

"Thanks for watching over her while I handled my business, sis. You can leave now if you want."

Queen and Chime looked at one another. Queen was up to something. "Can I take Chime to her house to get her clothes and see her family?" She asked, shocking me since she wasn't the friendly type. Speaking up for Chime let me know they'd been bonding. It was now going on two weeks since she'd been here.

I understood what my sister was trying to do, and Chime could use a female ear. I wanted Chime to feel comfortable around us. "No, you can take her shopping. It's cool." I told her to keep it real.

"I'm glad. You don't mind us using that black card, either, right?" Queen asked.

I shook my head and looked through my mail. Before leaving for the day, I had to pay a few bills and employees. My time was always limited. It felt like I had shit to do every second of my life. I didn't mind, because I felt like a man should always be busy.

"I said go head. Now y'all can leave." I spoke nonchalantly, not giving a fuck how I came off. I was done with that conversation; other things needed to be done.

I looked to see my sister drop her head, but she left my office. The only person left standing before me was Chime.

Chime's hair was in tight curls coming down past her shoulders a little. Shawty was wearing an all-black bodysuit, something I was sure my sister talked her into. On top of her bodysuit, she wore a green vest to match her heels. I could get used to this shit. I'd never seen Chime dressed this way. I don't even think she knew how sexy she looked. I had to look away because my dick was getting hard. I placed my hands on my lap to calm my partner down.

She noticed my shit was hard. I couldn't help it. It was

obvious I was attracted to her. Chime walked closer to my desk, and I could see the makeup on her face. She must have done it. My sister was never really into makeup. Queen was hard on showing natural beauty, so she wouldn't dare.

"What can I do for you, ma?" I asked, focusing on Chime's face, especially the shade of lip gloss covering her lips. Everything down to the perfume she was wearing had a nigga hyped. If a nigga didn't know any better, I would say shawty was trying to seduce me.

Chime walked around and sat on top of my desk directly in front of me. This damn girl had the nerve to place one leg on each side of my chair. Her pussy was directly in front of my face. If only she knew she was playing a dangerous game. I wanted to show this young ass girl what she wanted, but it would mess her head up and show her a thing or two about the game she wanted to play.

I didn't let her have her moment. Hell, I was already enjoying it too much. If this was her way of getting me to do what she wanted, she was close. She almost had a nigga gone.

"I need your full attention. I want to see my family over the weekend, even if it's just for five minutes. You don't understand what this is doing to me." She was almost in tears, but I couldn't let that shit get to a nigga.

I pushed my chair back and stood up. I reached my hand out to help Chime off my desk. She declined my hand and jumped down, walking straight out of my office without saying a word. At least she got the picture. A nigga already had plans for us this weekend.

"Women!" I yelled.

This shit was crazy. Chime threw the same fit my sister did, yet I was the only one to get my way. They had to get a better approach when coming to me.

Chapter Seven

Major Brown

It was hard to be there for my baby mama with all the shit my family had going on. We had our own life to manage and trying to manage my lifestyle and relationship was hard. My baby mama always thought a nigga was out fucking around on her. That had never been the case. Shawty has been keeping me satisfied on every level for years, so she had nothing to worry about.

I had been gone all weekend, and my baby mama was gonna snap when I got home. I thought I was playing it cool, trying to wait until she went to work, but as soon as I walked into my house, she jumped out on a nigga.

"Oh, so we're sneaking around this bitch nowadays?" Kesha snapped, throwing a nigga off. She must have been looking out the window all night 'cause my living room was set up like a stakeout.

"I don't have time for this shit, Key. You know where the fuck I've been and who I've been with."

I kept that shit short and sweet. I wasn't in any mood to go back and forth with her. I needed my sleep. I'd been up for two days and was starting to see and hear shit that wasn't there. So much bullshit went down this last week that I was trying to regroup from. Being home was the only place I felt comfortable enough to do so.

I hoped she still had to work so I could be alone. My twins were in school, and my baby girl had been with Kesha's mother for the weekend. I couldn't wait to see my princesses.

I had three daughters. I was a lucky man. My oldest two girls were ten and a spitting image of me. The only thing they didn't have of mine was my eyes. They inherited eyes like my mother and brother. One day, their eyes would be gray and the next green. My great-grandmother passed down the pretty eyes to us because my brother had eyes like hers. Everything else about my daughters, Promise and Passion, was Kesha all day. My youngest baby girl looked like Kesha. She had her skin tone and all. My baby was a chocolate drop, and I loved it.

I could say she was daddy's little girl. She had a hold on a nigga like no other. Paris was just six months and rotten. She already had her cry game down pack. One way or another, she would get what she wanted and didn't have to cry. Once she was old enough to understand that, she'd use that to her advantage as her sisters and mother did.

My kids were spoiled to the point that the teacher and daycare hated seeing me come. They knew I didn't give a fuck whose fault it was. I was coming up to that school and daycare. Let my kids come home crying or call me or tell me something was wrong, and it would be another episode of *John Q* out this bitch. Nobody was safe. A motherfucker could play with my money before I'd let them play with them. Over my family and kids, I'd lay a nigga and a bitch down. I wasn't the type of father to not do for mine. I went over and beyond and went without it for a long time, so my family could have it all.

Even though Kesha had a job, I made her keep her money in her pocket. Outside of being the mother of my kids, she was also my best friend and the love of my life. Kesha was short as hell, four-foot-eleven with a brown skin tone. She was beautiful in every way. She was thick to death. I loved every inch of her two-hundred-and-sixty-pound body. She gave a nigga like me life, plus she was wifey. My baby was good on and off her feet. She owned her hair studio on Wall Street in Louisiana. It took her a few years, but she got her own.

Kesha had a hair studio and did nails and makeup on the side. She was independent and good on her own. Yet, I still gave her money. She used to get mad when I made her take it. She never wanted me to feel she was using me, and I didn't. I wanted her to stop working, but she laughed me off.

A nigga paid all the bills, both our car notes, and the daycare bill. It was nothing for me to play my part and not cheat. She only had to worry about her gambling habits, which were out of control, but fuck it. I never wanted shit from her, but her love, trust, and loyalty. Kesha took me off the market, and it'd been that way for ten years.

"Do you miss me? I mean, we don't talk or even text anymore. Is there someone else?" she quizzed.

I stopped Kesha right in her tracks by pulling her to me. I placed my finger over her lips and kissed them. As I took off her clothes, I let my tongue dance in her mouth. Kesha knew better than to ask that. Nobody was getting this dick and head from me but Kesha. There was too much sick shit out there. When a man was happy at home, it was just that.

I pulled the white tee shirt she had on over her head, exposing her beautiful ass breasts. They popped right out, looking me dead in the face like they were happy to see a nigga. I jumped right into it, placing her right nipple in my mouth. All the fight left her when I started to suck on her breasts. Her body jumped from the anticipation alone.

"Yes, baby, right, their daddy! Mm, mm, that's it." She cooed in a nigga's ear as I licked both of her nipples.

My tongue roamed every spot open on her body. I picked her up like it was nothing and carried her to our bedroom. The whole time I walked, I had my tongue dead in her mouth. She knew she said a mouthful when she asked if there was someone else. She wanted me to beat it up and remind her she was the only one for me. That's why she stayed home.

I placed Kesha down on the bed and pulled her boy shorts off. I opened her legs as wide as I could get them. Once I got them where I needed them, I dove in. Her body started shaking, causing me to lick deeper and suck harder.

"Ssshiitttt! I'm fucking cumming so hard, bae. Mm, why do you do this to me?" she asked.

I didn't say a word, because I had a mouthful of delicious pussy to deal with. I placed three fingers inside her pussy and went to work.

Shawty's body sat straight up off the bed once she felt my tongue hit that clit. "Oh yes, baby! That's it. I see Jesus! My God!"

All I could do was laugh. Kesha did all this before I slid inside her. When Kesha got the dick, I would have her speaking in tongues. I replaced my fingers with my dick in one swift move. We both let out a moan as I started stroking her slowly. I didn't even have my full dick in her, and Kesha called herself trying to run seconds after I started hitting it.

I pulled her body as close as it could get to me, then drilled the fuck out of her mouthy ass. I watched my dick go in and out of her juicy pussy. Every stroke had a nigga ready to bust, but she would say I came fast and was cheating. I pulled out and flipped her over. My baby arched her back just like she knew daddy liked it. So turned on, I smashed my dick inside her, hitting her from the back and slapping her thick ass at the same time.

I felt her juices coming down my leg, which only made a nigga go crazy. I placed one of her legs up and started doing tricks in that pussy. She started to tap out and run, but I pulled her to me and held her in the position I needed her in. I was sure our lovemaking could be heard from the hallway.

"Oh, shit, I feel it, baby. It's in my ribs," she called out, hyping me up.

I fucked Kesha harder and faster, feeling myself about to nut. I slowed down and came to a complete stop. She knew what time it was. I laid back so she could ride a nigga home.

"Come let me taste it first," I demanded.

Kesha did as I said, and I put her ass to sleep from the head.

∞∞∞

"Good morning, can I help you with something?" A funny-looking white girl asked, trying to stop me from attending my meeting.

I ignored the lady at the front desk question, because she should have been up on game on who I was. We were meeting with the dog breeder to see how our dogs were making out at the Louisiana dog pound. We also had dogs with a New York breeder, which was where these ones would go once they reached a healthy weight. Breeding them was more challenging than we expected. It took us all of ten weeks to get them to the weight we needed them at. Now I had the paperwork of eight and buyers for all, so it was time to trade money for dogs.

I wasn't dressed as if I belonged in a place like this. None of that mattered once you were an owner. Little did she know, this was my building. I may not be here often due to the new companies we've started, which meant she was just familiar with my sister Queen.

I was here to finish up paperwork, so I ignored her question and showed myself the way. I walked past her to my office to where the meeting would be held. There would be a lot of important motherfuckers at this meeting. I was one of them now. My brothers and I were the proud owners of our own security business, which we were doing out of this building, too. Discussing the security business was also the point of this meeting.

"Sir, please, before I call the authorities, I'm telling you that you can't go in there," the white girl stressed. As I reached the door to open it, she pulled on me.

"Mary, what are you doing to Mr. Brown?" One gentleman I was there to meet asked.

She looked at me and then at him. I guessed him telling her my name rang a bell, 'cause now the bitch was fixing my clothes. I got the respect from her now, that she needed to have when I walked in.

"I'm so sorry, sir. I had no clue you were, Mr. Brown. Please accept my apologies."

I smiled, walked past her, and took my seat. I had forty-five minutes before I had to leave to meet Kesha. My phone went off with a text from my baby mama the second her name came to mind. I looked down at the picture I had saved with her and our kids and couldn't do shit but smile. As the meeting began, I sat back in my chair.

"I'm glad we all could make it today. Now let's get down to the topic of the day." Prince was straightforward and started the meeting the same way all the time.

I was proud to call him my little brother. He made shit happen. Even when we were young, he played the fatherly role. At first, it felt like a little brother taking care of the big brothers. He did as he should, because we couldn't. That's what family was for, and I would be forever grateful. My brother held me down when I got locked up. Prince didn't even let us pay him back for anything he did for us.

"So that wraps up the meeting for this week. Get with one another and discuss what you need to and come back to me with numbers." Prince finished up and walked off.

King and I followed Prince. I had ten minutes before I had to step off. This was just the start of my day. My next meeting was twenty minutes away. Good thing everything was not too far from Louisiana, where I resided. I had meetings all morning, but before that, my daughter had a father/daughter breakfast, and I wouldn't miss that for the world.

I walked into Prince's office. "I can't stay. I got to meet the twins for breakfast."

I could see he was in a better mood. Bruh had been going through it but never would show the stress. He was the one keeping us all together. We tried to be there for him, but the nigga thought he was God.

"Go 'head, man. Kiss my nieces for me," Prince stated.

"No doubt."

I left both my brothers in the room. They would be good without me today. This day was for my twins' day. I pulled into my house and felt my head spinning. Kesha was supposed to be at work, but she was home. Plus, there was a black SUV parked behind her car. Without hesitation, I grabbed my gun, exited my car, and raced to the house.

I touched the door, checking to see if it was locked. It was wide open. So help me, God, Kesha had better have been here with a bitch and not a nigga. They both would die today, and my kids would be motherless. I told her I was coming home, but since I had been away so much lately, she probably thought I wouldn't make it home for this breakfast and invited her nigga over. She kept saying I was the one cheating, but maybe it was her. They say everything happens for a reason, so I figured I was about to find out if this was a sneak attack or not.

I walked right into the front door with my gun already aimed. I could hear a child and another female's voice. It had to be one of Kesha's friends or clients. I put my gun away since I knew it was a bitch.

"Baby, who the fuck truck is that?" I asked, walking into my living room and seeing the last person I wanted to see on earth — my ex-girlfriend and first love, Makayla, who also was Kesha's ex-best friend.

"H-heyyy b-baeee." Kesha stuttering and shit like she was shocked to see me.

I looked over at Makayla and then at the little girl beside her. "Long time no see, Makayla. What brings you by after eleven years?" I joked, but I was sure they made up and wanted to rekindle their friendship.

I couldn't help but keep eyeing the little girl down. Shit, I wanted to say she looked just like my twins. She had the same eyes, complexion, and all. Who was she fucking that I didn't know about back then?

"She came to see you about something. I'll let you both talk, maybe catch up a little." Kesha stated with her arms crossed. She looked a little hurt about having to say that much to me. Kesha walked off with tears in her eyes, making me want to call out for her. Now, I needed to know what the fuck was bugging her.

"What's up? Why are you here?" I asked Makayla.

"This here is Imani Aaliyah. I'd like you to meet your daughter," Makayla announced.

I must have been hearing shit. I could have sworn she said *daughter*. "I'm hearing shit, because it sounds like you said my daughter."

Kesha came out of the cut. "She did, baby, and I should have stayed in here with you to hear this all." I had to look twice because Kesha was crying harder.

"Why did you wait eleven years, Makayla? On your own time

as always!" I snapped, but it did me no good. I had a daughter who I didn't know about. I missed all of her life, and that wasn't fair.

"I was hurt you ran off with my best fucking friend. How would that conversation come about? Y'all would have thought I wanted you to stay."

I wasn't trying to hear that shit. There still was no excuse. As for Kesha, she may have taken it there with her. She wasn't trying to hear shit after the fallout. She wanted her head for talking about her dad back then. My baby used to be about that hood life. Back then, she was truly my ride-or-die. I could say I made her chill out from all that hype. Unlike most niggas, I needed my girl to do something with herself. I had a reputation out there. So as for that fighting shit, I stopped that.

"I don't care what you say. I would have listened. You sent me pictures of that pussy after we broke up. You even reached out last year, sending me ass pictures. So, don't lie, you saved this information for what?" I grilled, and at the same time, I gave out too much.

I looked over at Makayla. To my surprise, the girl was sitting on my sofa and smiling.

Kesha's eyes were locked in on Makayla. "Oh, bitch, did you?" She asked, stepping over to Makayla, ready to rekindle their past beef. I had to step in, because baby girl didn't need to see any of this. Kesha pushed me off and left the room on my ass, leaving me to deal with the devil alone.

"What's your name, little mama?" I asked the little girl.

She looked at me and smiled. "I'm Imani. What's your name, sir?" her cute, sweet ass said.

I couldn't let the sweet talk get me yet. I needed to get a blood test first. "My name is Major, and it's nice to finally meet you." I told her. She had a nigga's heart melting already.

"Mommy says you're my father. Is this true?"

I looked over at Makayla's ass, and she looked away. She'd had better be looking for Kesha. Her whole being here was more than what she came for. This was harder on Kesha than it was on me. She would think this girl wanted me back.

Meanwhile, I thought she wanted money from me. Nevertheless, I felt bad for the little girl. I could only imagine what she had been through with Makayla. I wanted to know everything about her life. I had a lot of catching up to do. I would even go as far as letting them stay with me until the test was done, but I knew Kesha wouldn't be down with that.

"Can I stay with you? Mommy's boyfriend scared me, and you seem like a nice man already." When she said that, I wanted to fuck her mother up for having any man around her who she was uncomfortable with.

"Okay, let's go. I have a hotel up on 8th Street. I will be here for a week. I'm in room 212. I can leave you my cell phone number. Let me know when you are ready to test Imani." Makayla grabbed baby girl and headed out the door.

I didn't stop her. There was nothing I could do just yet. Already, I hated the look she gave me as she left. As soon as she walked out, shots went off.

Makayla got down, but I had to race for baby girl, who was halfway to the car. She didn't even get down. She stood there, unaware of what was happening. Once I reached her, I pulled her to the ground and shot my gun back. I got up and fired four more times, running in the car's direction.

It was the same car that ran Prince off the road the other day. I read the license plate number on the car. I would send that shit to my boy to run the tags. If I were lucky, I could see if the shit had a GPS. I would pull the fuck up at his front door if I could locate him. The car was gone in the wind when I let off the last shot.

I looked around, making sure all was well. Baby girl was good. No harm was done to her or Makayla. I pulled baby girl close to me and helped Makayla up as well. I made them come back to the house 'cause I needed them under my protection. I wanted to kill this nigga today because he was out of line.

It was a problem any time niggas felt comfortable enough to come to where I rested my head. Niggas were too comfortable with this being the second time they attempted to kill us, only they came for me alone this time.

I was sure Peanut was the shooter. It was me who nearly killed him so it's only right. I reached my porch and lost my fucking mind. Kesha was laid out bleeding from the chest. She must have come out when she heard the gunfire. I felt a part of me leave earth.

"Call 911! Hurry up!" I ordered Makayla.

Makayla called for help, then rushed to my side to help stop the blood.

Chapter Eight

Cinnamon Smith

I was waiting on my little sister to get all she knew about this Prince Brown guy to me. I may not have been in the streets, but I knew my way around them. They made it seem like I was stuck up and hard to deal with, pretty much the same story one of my sisters told our entire life. It was like I wasn't good enough to be Chance's sister when all I'd ever wanted was the best for both of them. Chime and Chance were all I had left. Outside of my daughter, London, they were who I lived for.

Finally, Chance found the information we needed. I knew someone who could help us that I used to deal with. We had to end our sexual relationship, because he was a dog running free. Well, he wasn't exactly free, because I married the dog. Now I needed his assistanc and to pick up the child we shared.

I pulled in at his job and parked next to him. Leaving Chance in the car, I walked inside, waved at his secretary, and kept it moving. All I had was twenty minutes to get in and get out since I had one pit stop to make.

When I reached the third floor, I knocked lightly on his door and let myself into my husband's office. He was in the middle of pleasing his assistant, as usual. Linda saw me, jumped up, got dressed, and left.

"Hi, honey." I said as she closed the door behind her.

Mark was six-foot-two and about two hundred and ten pounds. He was light skin with brown eyes and no tats, scars, or anything. I used to go crazy over this man. Now, he just drove me crazy. I took my seat in front of his desk as he fixed himself. I handed him the paper with everything about Prince on it.

"Hello, my ass, you're late picking up London. She had to hear that poor lady yell from daddy fucking her good like I used to do you, remember?"

Mark made my skin crawl. He had me messed up for having my baby listening to him having sex. I didn't have time for his shit. I let what he said go in one ear and out the other. He always made passes at me, but I would never return to him.

As he pulled up the information, I sat back and didn't say a word. I needed a location on that phone and now. He printed it out and tried to hug me when I stood up, but I popped him. I wasn't going for it this time. I would never regret my child, but I regretted the timing of having her. She was here, and I was good. I just should have never married him.

Mark called out to my four-year-old daughter. "Let's go, London, baby. Mommy's here, and I have to go. I don't have all day."

I hated that Mark would even say that to her. His being busy had nothing to do with her. "Take your time. He could leave. We know the way out," I called out to my daughter.

London came out of the lounge area he had in his office as if we had just woken her up. Her hair was pulled back in a ponytail. She had just gone shopping with her dad yesterday, so her outfit was brand new.

"Did you spend time with her at all? Or is this the work of your mother?" I asked.

London came to me with her head down. As I kissed her cheek, I grabbed her bag off the wall, and searched through it. Looking through the bag and seeing everything nice and neat let me know my daughter had been with her grandmother, which was fine. I knew she would be well taken care of.

"Look, my mother and girlfriend had the child. She was fine. She woke up thirty minutes ago. My mom let her stay up and watch scary movies again," he said.

It hurt to know they had gotten careless with her. It started when I'd have to work overnight. London had to stay with her, and I kept telling her repeatedly not to let her stay up past eight or nine. Come to find out, she'd be up all night and would sleep in daycare all day. I wasn't hard on her. She could stay up sometimes. I allowed it once a week, but it lacked parenting to do it every day of the month.

Mark frowned. "Lock up when you all are done. I have shit to do." He left his office not knowing this was the last time he would see his daughter.

"Mommy, my back is itching. Can you stop it?" London cried out.

I went into Mark's bathroom, which had a shower, started the water, and tested it. After making sure it was just right for her to get in, I pulled London's clothes off and helped her into her shower. Right away, I saw marks and bruises. I jumped, holding my mouth in disbelief.

"Baby, what happened to your body, honey? Who did this to you?" I asked my daughter. Her body looked so worn out. I thought she was groggy from not sleeping, but it was from being abused.

London's wide eyes filled with hurt as she answered me. "Mommy, grandma drinks and hits me when she gets mad."

I pulled my daughter out of the shower, wet and all, and hugged her. I had no clue why she didn't tell me her grandma was hitting her like this. I would never forgive myself. My daughter was half-loved by his side of the family, and his mother topped it off with physical abuse.

I sat on the bathroom floor and cried my eyes out for half an hour, to where my sister had to come in looking for me.

"Cinn, where are you?" Chance called out. I was so fucked up from all this I forgot she was outside.

"I'm in here. Come look at London, sis," I called out, crying again.

As soon as Chance saw her body, she dropped to the floor and joined me in crying. My sister loved my daughter, so I was sure this hurt her, too. This wasn't acceptable, not one bit.

"Come here, let me take pictures. We are going to the cops," I said.

Chance looked over at me like I was crazy. I wondered if she had a better idea of how to resolve this.

"You can go to the cops. I'm going to his house. How are we going to the cops going to help us? Look around. He's one of them. That's why he doesn't care," Chance reminded me.

"It wasn't him. It was his mother," I simply said. I didn't know what else to say or do.

After we did what we needed, I let my daughter shower. I put her clothes on and carried her to my car. London didn't have to ever worry about seeing that family again.

∞∞∞

The next morning, I woke up with the same crazy-ass dude standing over my bed. This time he wasn't holding a gun to my head, and Chime was behind him. I didn't know if I should jump up and hug her or not. I didn't move an inch since I was scared this man would kill me. I knew things with Prince were good, but I was still cautious.

I looked at my sister, who looked completely different. She

was dressed nicely, and the outfit suited her. For Chime to have been kidnapped, she was being treated great. Prince came back over by himself the next day to get the drugs in the vest and said the money was ours because Chime was working with his team to recover his losses and more.

I was mad Chance didn't step up when we got confronted about the dope and dog going missing. She had done something wild. I just didn't think she would take it from Prince.

Chance took more than she needed, something noticeable. Leave it up to her to go overboard. Not to sound hypocritical, being as though I wasn't at all innocent. I blamed myself just as much as I blamed Chance. I wanted to pull my hair out when they took Chime. My mind was racing to figure out why we had such bad luck.

I smiled so wide as London laid eyes on Chime.

"Chime, is that you? Are you okay?" I asked

"It's okay, sis. He let me come to see you, because I missed you guys," Chime assured me, making me feel better.

She was fine, and I needed to hear that. Still, I wanted more, though. I needed her back home today. This was a lot to take in. I needed my family. This couldn't be life. If it was, why was life hitting us this hard?

Life sucked for us, and it was my fault. They wouldn't understand why I felt it was my fault. I am the reason my mom left us. I lost her love child. My mom and grandmother were gone, and now Prince snatched Chime. When would it be our turn to win in life? I stopped attending church, because I didn't think God wanted to hear from me. I was the reason my sister went missing, the reason my mom left us, and the reason I couldn't protect my daughter.

"Mommy, I'm scared," London cried out. She probably remembered when Prince was here last time.

"Don't be scared, London. I just wanted to check on you guys. Aunty is at work now, so I can visit you," Chime said, encouragingly.

Something else was different about Chime than just her appearance, but I couldn't put my finger on it. I didn't say anything, but I noticed it. My relationship with Chime wasn't as smooth as it could be. Chance thought our disconnect was that I didn't want them to grow up, but I had my reasons.

"I'ma let y'all talk. I'll be outside, ma," Prince stated, and that's when it hit me. It was him and her that was different. There was a connection, and I could see it. That says things happen for a reason. I hope that's true.

Once Prince was gone, Chime raced over to me. I held her as she cried. That was the Chime I knew. She was trying to be strong and not show Prince any weakness. "Where is Chance? I needed to ask her something?" she asked.

That was a good question. Chance would usually be here. I hoped she didn't go to London's grandmother's house.

"She may be out looking for London's grandmother. Something went down over the weekend, but we are fine," I assured her.

I was glad Chime came to visit as she promised. I needed this. To see my sister cry broke me. I wanted to break down and call on the Lord. Hopefully, that will save us. With the way my luck and blessings were set up, I needed to try to hope and cross my fingers.

"Listen to me closely. I will be staying with Prince for a while, working with him to clear up the debt we owe him for what Chance did, but I will be fine. Trust me. If I need you guys, I will text you. I'm okay. I promise," Chime said.

I hated to see her leave and go back under Prince's rule, but she actually looked happy. "Okay, Chime. I love you. Be safe, and see you soon," I expressed.

As soon as we hugged again, Prince was knocking on my room door. "Sorry to break things up, but let's go." His mean ass was mad. From what I heard, he was always making jokes, but he didn't seem to have a sense of humor right then.

London hugged Chime and broke down. I looked over at Prince, and his ass looked away. I was in disbelief that he had the heart to begin with. His mood shifted as his phone went off. He walked out to take the call.

"Baby, your aunty will see you later. She's coming home soon." I assured my daughter with a hug.

As we broke apart, my door swung open.

"Oh my God, Chime!" Chance cried out, and they both ran to one another.

Prince let my sisters have their moment, because Chance had just got here. They held each other and cried like they hadn't seen each other in years. I pretty much felt the same way.

Out of nowhere, they started speaking in a different language. That's what they used to do back when they were kids when they didn't want us to know what they were saying. It was called pig Latin, and you had to be cool to know what they were talking about. My sister spoke that shit so fast that it lost me. I could make out some words. Others I didn't even try.

"Hold on with that talk. I can't understand the shit y'all saying. Y'all might be trying to set a nigga up." Prince halted their reunion as he motioned for Chime.

Chime looked at him with the same eyes she gave us when she wanted to get her way. He shook his head and walked out of the room. She continued talking to Chance, still holding on to London.

"He must like you, because you don't look kidnapped. You're

dressed differently in some shit I would wear. Look at you glowing and shit," Chance joked.

Chime didn't laugh. She looked busted, or like she had to tell us something. She looked down to hide her smile every time we spoke his name. I bet money that she and Prince had something going on.

"It's nothing like that. He's my boss now, remember?" Chime shot back, making Chance damn laugh.

"Let's go." A big dude came to my bedroom door talking to Chime. I figured Prince got sick of begging her, so he sent the big guy. Behind him was another big guy holding onto a gun. I was guessing Prince was the boss of them all. He must have been that man to be because he had men my age working for him.

Prince stepped into the room and looked at Chime. "Okay, we gotta go, baby. Hug and kiss your family." He said before walking away again.

I was stuck on him calling my sister baby. I wondered if he slipped up and said that or if they had something going on.

"Now that y'all are in love in shit, I should tell you it was me who took the money and the dog, not my sister. Okay, Prince, and I'm sorry," Chance called out.

He just smiled and winked at her. "I knew that all along. You were the only one connected to my shit. You can keep the dog. I got my product. Chime is still working off the audacity you had."

Chance raced to her closet, pulled down the money she had gotten off the card, and handed it over. Prince dropped it on the floor and walked out of the room.

As soon as he stepped away, the atmosphere in the room lit up. The guys were big and scary, and they walked off with Prince.

"I love you guys. Stop beating yourself up. We're fine," Chime reminded us.

Prince walked back in. "Just because I'm feeling Chime don't mean you should get me fucked up. Make no mistake about it. When I tell you ladies, don't try that shit again, I mean it. Don't let this visit get to your head. I won't be so nice the next time you cross me." He walked out, leaving me and Chance lost for words.

"I hope that's his way of welcoming us to the family." I joked as we laughed.

Chapter Nine

Lyric

Prince didn't think I knew what he had going on, but I did. A few days after we got back from our trip, I hadn't seen or heard from him. Prince had been ignoring my calls, and when I came to the stash house, they had changed up the code to get in on my ass. Like any other bitch, I wanted to know about my man, so I popped the fuck up on his ass. Yeah, I got it. He had a lot going on, but not that much for him to push me off to the side. Not the one person who, as far as he knew, held him down so he could be free to get everything he had today.

Word on the street was that he had new help up in that bitch. I wanted to see what kind of help his ass had, 'cause they weren't helping me get to him. When I found out who it was, I knew I would have to beat her ass. Prince knew better than to act like this. It usually was me that pushed him away. Now that he was fucking with Chime. He done grew some balls on a bitch. Not saying he didn't have balls before. He wasn't soft. I was just his soft spot.

I dialed his number as I followed behind his ass. There was no more running he could do. He had done all that talk about the twins, only for me to find out he had the bitch working for him. I could see if he killed her. That would be the proper punishment. That's what he does to the niggas that take from him. Why go easy on a bitch? There was no justification for it other than his real feelings for Chime. I couldn't understand why he had been feeling her for years.

When I spotted Chime and Queen out shopping, I thought

I was seeing shit. I followed them around just to hear what they would talk about. I found out all I needed to know. I felt like this was a joke he wanted to play with a bitch. Then Prince ignored my calls after saying he couldn't talk because he was missing his money. That day, I followed Queen and Chime to see where Chime lived, only to find out Prince had the bitch stashed at his spot. Queen was a trader, and Prince would end up in jail for good this time. I just had to help get him there.

I was going to win back my man or send him away for good. This time, I would put Slime on for real. Things were rocky with Slime. He was bipolar and crazy all in one. We were in the honeymoon stage for one minute, and everything was good. The next minute, he was choking the life out of me. Did I love Slime? It was nothing like that. It was more so I loved how I could make him do shit, because he loved me.

I dialed Prince's number one more time. He was going to have to talk to me.

"Why do you keep blowing my phone up? I told you I've been busy!" Prince snapped on a bitch as soon as he answered.

I had to look down at the phone to make sure I had the right number. It sounded like I was talking to Slime. Prince had never spoken to me like that. He had so much more respect for females. I could tell he was pissed at me by the tone of his voice.

"Don't act like I'm bothering you, nigga. Damn, you've been around that twin and don't know how to talk to me anymore. You must have fucked her." I joked, but I was the only one to find that shit funny. That made me burn with envy inside. Prince and Chime were about to get their feelings hurt. I wasn't about to come second to this bitch.

"You ain't calling to talk about shit 'cause you messy. Your attention is on shawty, not me," he stated, and he was correct for the most part.

I needed to know why my man was always around her and when she would go home. Understanding Prince's feelings for Chime made it easy to understand why he moved her in right away. It also was clear that he had pushed me to the side.

"You ain't seen messy yet. Don't worry, though. I'm finna pull up!" I yelled, hanging up so fast. I was mad and jealous and hated it when I snapped like that. I would say anything out of my mouth. Prince knew better than to try me like that, and he knew how far I would go for his ass.

Following him at a distance to his stash house, I stayed two cars behind, because I didn't want to be seen and mess up my pop-up. There was no doubt in my mind they had something going on with how he treated me.

I waited for Prince to go into the house before I pulled in. I hopped over the fence and jogged to the door. Waiting for the camera to go around, I punched in the code. Prince forgot I helped his ass set up this house, mapped out his man cave and all. Thankfully, the master code worked like a charm every time.

I hurried over to his talking computer to make sure it didn't give me away. Seconds after someone walked in, she would greet them. I programmed that too, so I knew how to disarm it. I left the entryway and went straight to the main office. I had passed two rooms and a bathroom before entering the office to find Chime and Queen eating lunch. The bitch looked happy as hell to be in my man's house. This was crazy. Knowing Chime stole from him, he had her all up in his house like this.

"Well, damn, Queen, you have a new best friend, I see." I sassed to Queen, letting my appearance be known. They looked up as if they had seen a ghost or some shit.

Queen moved closer to me as if she were about to hug me. "Why are you here? Does my brother know?" she asked.

Her question only pissed me off more. Why the fuck would

she ask me that in front of this bitch? She was playing me to the left. Queen knew how hard it was for me to get in the house. Everything I went through with him she knew about, and it hurt. Now she was throwing it in my face, and I didn't like that.

"I'm his girl. I don't need to tell him when I want to see him!" I snapped at this point.

There was nothing left to discuss with Queen. She acted differently in front of Chime, almost like she took my place in her life. To see them laughing and joking and having a good time at the mall hurt me. Queen could act funny all she wanted. I would tell her brother the truth about us since she thought this shit was sweet.

"I just let my brother know you were here, and he said to go to his office. Other than that, I have nothing to say until you grow up." Queen shot back at me.

"Well, let's see what Prince has to say when I tell him about our friendship." I threatened, snapping my head to the side on her ass. She looked like she wanted to fight when I gave her the *now what* stare.

"Go to hell!" Queen yelled.

"I'll see you there." I tossed over my shoulder as I left the room and headed toward Prince's office. I opened the door and walked in to see he wasn't happy to see me.

"When have I ever been okay with you popping the fuck up on me?" he asked.

I ignored his question, acting like I did nothing wrong, and sat on his lap. I was happy to see he didn't push me off. That alone would tell me what kind of mood he was in. It took me a few minutes to answer because I was making shit up in my head to say. I needed to come big or stay home with this lie. I took my hand and started playing with the print in his pants, which made my pussy wet as hell. I wanted him badly.

Prince's sex was off the chain to the point where people didn't understand what I'd do for that dick. He didn't give head, but his dick game made up for it. Prince not giving head pretty much would have been a deal-breaker if he didn't know how to fuck.

"I need you to just let me taste him, baby. She needs his attention." I cooed.

He pushed his chair back and allowed me to kneel in front of him. I dropped to my knees and unzipped his pants, releasing his beast of manhood. At attention already, his dick had a bitch's mouth watering and ready for it. I only had one goal: to please this motherfucker's every need.

Prince held his dick in his hand, waving it back and forth, teasing me. He stood to his feet and smacked me in the face with his dick. That shit turned me on like he knew it would.

I was ready for what he was about to do next as he held his dick to my mouth and spoke, "Suck this dick so you can get the fuck out. This is all you wanted anyway, so come on."

There was something about how Prince spoke to me. I loved it when he told me what to do and how to please him. Most women didn't like that kind of control. As for me, I loved it. Talk shit to my ass, and I'd fuck you better. I wanted it nasty, so as the word suck rolled off his lips, my pussy juices started flowing water for him. Making me put his manhood in my mouth, I damned near choked on it.

I spat on Prince's dick and took the full ten inches in my mouth, just how he liked it while looking his fine ass dead in the face. As I sucked him off, I reached down, lifted my dress, and opened my legs. I placed three fingers in my pussy while going crazy on the dick.

Prince put his hand on the back of my head and guided my head up and down. I sucked the hell outta his dick, giving him the best head that I had in me, yet this nigga didn't make a sound. I used my tongue to roll around the tip of his dick, making my mouth water only to go deeper down on his dick. Sucking on the head of his dick while moaning, I tried to get this nigga to at least make a sound to let me know he was into it.

I loved everything about this man, and he was pulling away from me. I couldn't explain why I had done him wrong. Prince was fine as he wanted to be. He put me in mind of my favorite rapper Dave East. Dave East's sexy ass could get it raw just so I could have his babies. Prince and the rapper Dave East could pass as twins. The two favored so much that they had to be related down the line.

Prince's fine ass had these bitches going crazy, not just over his looks but that dick and green eyes. Man, he was the most wanted hood nigga. His goatee was a turn-on. I had a thing for niggas with a goatee. His money was just a bonus and a good one. I used to say he and I made the perfect match. My attitude was a little off, but it matched him, and that's all that matters.

"Suck that dick, ma. Wet it up," Prince coached, making me show off.

When I left here, he would be following me. As I sucked his tip to his balls, I got wetter and wetter, ready for him to enter me. I wasn't sure why he was taking so long to fuck me, or why he hadn't made a sound as I pleased him. It made me feel like I wasn't fully satisfying him. Prince just sat there, making occasional commands for me to suck harder.

On the other hand, I always went all out for Prince in bed. I gave my all every time we fucked. I made sure I never made the same move twice. Yet, he acted as if my little booty wasn't hitting.

Finally, after a long time of trying, he dropped his kids off in my mouth. I couldn't tell he was coming at first, because he was so quiet. Had it not been for his eyes rolling in the back of his head, I would've stopped since that was all I could get out of him. Prince left me there looking crazy as he headed to the bathroom. He didn't even watch me swallow his kids like he usually did. I didn't know what to think of us. Still, I had to be doing something right, because I was the one in his office pleasing him, not Chime.

Prince finished up in the bathroom. I fixed my clothes and sat there, about to plan dinner and a movie. Prince had me so weak that I couldn't let him go. I had to have everything about him: his attention, time, and last name.

When he returned from the bathroom, I was still in a trance from sucking his dick. I was mad, though. I wondered why this fuck session was just about him getting pleased. "So, I can't have any dick?"

"Oh, nawl. You fucked that up by running your mouth and popping up on a nigga." He walked up to me and extended his hand. Prince helped me get up off the floor and fixed the buckle on his pants.

I sucked my teeth and rolled my eyes. I was about to reply when someone knocked on the door and said, "Hey, are you busy?"

I smiled as I waited to see her face now that I was back in the picture. I sat next to Prince on his desk, making it look good.

Prince called out, "Come in."

Ms. Chime cleaned up nicely. Her hair and makeup were on point. She wore a Gucci outfit. Her beauty caught me off my game when she walked in. I almost asked if my man had bought it for her. We all knew this wasn't how she dressed. Fuck that, the airport wasn't paying that well, so I knew Prince and Queen tag-teamed this bitch in. I couldn't say what I wanted to right then. I didn't want to do too much for Prince to send me home. I had to fake like he ran shit when we were around people.

"You good, ma? What's up?" Prince asked, looking innocent like I didn't just have him all down my throat.

"I just wanted to get some air with Queen. Is that okay?"

Chime asked as if she needed permission. The girl had the nerve to be hurt about something.

I grinned hard, making sure she saw me smile.

Prince said nothing. He just looked at her. The way he looked at her had my mind spinning. It was as if he felt bad about something.

I stood and walked closer to Prince. I sat in his lap and opened my mouth for him since he couldn't say a word. "Go ahead. We have business to handle, hun."

Prince broke out of his thoughts and gave her the *I wanna fuck* eyes. For Prince to stare at her like I wasn't in the room pissed me off. We didn't have an official title, but everyone knew that was me. I was sick of running hoes off. It had been a battle trying to keep him interested. The only way to keep his mind off the next bitch was to make sure she didn't have one up on me. Chime changing her whole style for him didn't make the first difference. I knew something she didn't know, and that was every weak spot he had on his body.

Prince ignored what I said to Chime. "She was just leaving. We're done for the day, so I can take you myself."

I was ten seconds off from killing them both. Everything Prince spoke out of his mouth was fucked up. He had the nerve to flirt right in front of me. It was crazy how all the bitches he met knew how I was coming but this one. Prince was a natural flirt, always complimenting these hoes, and they thought anything he did was sexy. He could just nod his head at a female and set them off. All this to say, I hated how he was giving Chime more attention than I got.

Deep down, I may have been jealous. I was in love with him, so everything he did worked on my nerves. When it came to fucking me, he knew his way around my body. His dick game was from God himself. Prince was blessed in the dick department. So,

I had a reason to trip on him when I did. The thought of him even wanting Chime in a sexual way fucked with me. I could see in his eyes that something was there for her.

"So, you pushing me off for this girl? Who stole from you?" I snapped, standing to my feet. I was lost as to why he wanted to play with a bitch.

"How many times do I tell you to stay out of my business?" Prince roared.

I took a deep breath. "Too many times to count, but that doesn't matter."

His face switched up. One thing Prince hated was a smart-talking female. I low-key thought it turned him on at times. The only time he fucked me hard was when I'd talk my shit. I missed those days, because talking shit hadn't gotten me any good dick from him lately.

This conversation was pointless with him. He knew I was there but didn't pay me any attention. I got up and headed to the door to leave. I stood side by side with Chime, and the bitch didn't look my way.

"So, how long do I have to go without the dick?" I asked, annoyed that I had to go through this to get some. I felt like screaming out as the girl did in that *'it's my money, and I need it now'* commercial, except I would yell, *'it's my dick, and I need it now!'*

Prince looked me dead in the face with narrowed eyes. "Trust me when I tell you I know somebody's been giving you some dick. Why do you think I ain't fuck you just now? All a nigga let you do was suck this dick."

He knew too much, which scared me. I looked over at Chime in shock. She heard Prince degrade me, which only made me more upset.

Prince stood up and pulled his all-black hoodie over his head.

He had said a mouthful, which proved he was up to something, but what did he know? It didn't matter anymore. I did too much to him to care what he knew. It almost felt like a weight was lifted, but I had to keep the lie going.

"Baby, I'm only fucking you." I pushed past Chime.

Prince laughed out loud, making me swing around to see why. "You know what's so funny about that? Not only had I followed your ass one day, but I was surprised who dick I saw you sucking," he began.

I almost wanted to run. I started to walk away, but I wanted to hear the rest. So, I went ahead and entertained his conversation. "You saw me do what? Ha-ha," I fake laughed, waiting for more.

"You heard me. You should be happy I'm taking Chime out shopping to get some fresh air. She is the real reason you are still alive. You see, when I saw you in front of my stash house, I thought my eyes were playing tricks on a nigga," he relayed.

My heart dropped, because I was praying that Prince wasn't home or didn't see me, but he did, which meant he probably saw and heard it all. Prince had the kind of system where you could listen to a conversation.

"You have it all wrong. That wasn't me," I defended.

My lie only pissed Prince off to the point that he pulled his gun from his desk and sat it on the table. "Nawl, y'all had it all wrong, and I heard everything. So, tell me about the little girl named Harmony y'all have together?" Prince asked.

As soon as my daughter's name left his mouth, I pissed on myself right there and right then. I wanted to faint but didn't want to give him free access to kill my ass. As I stepped back into the hallway, waiting good and well until I was out the door, I took off running full speed to my car. I went out the same way I came in, almost falling to the ground. A bitch was running so fast that I didn't have time to look back and see shit. I was scared Prince would catch my ass. Once I got out the back door, I kept running to my car.

Hitting the unlock switch, I jumped right in. Pushing the push start button and dashing it, I didn't look back until I was clear out of the yard. That's when my phone rang. I picked it up from the car phone.

"You almost had me fooled, Lyric. Tell me how long you thought it would take me to find out you set me up?" Prince asked.

The tears started flowing. To say I was scared was an understatement. I knew what Prince was capable of. I didn't say shit. I just hung up. I could hear the hurt and hate in his voice. That was the last straw. There was no coming back from that. The safest thing for me to do was leave the state. I had to get my grandmother and my daughter out of the way. There was no telling what type of war I had just started. I wished I had thought this through before I started doing shit. I sat back, not sure where I was welcome to go. I lost my man and best friend on the same day.

"So, you mean to tell me that you were not only fucking me but also my brother and cousin? Damn Lyric, how are you going to fix this shit?" Queen asked from my back seat. She must have been hiding back there the whole time.

When I woke up today, I had a feeling it would be my last one. A person can feel when death is near. For the past four days, I have had bad dreams about dying, but I thought that was God telling me to slow my life down.

"Baby, it was nothing like that. Your cousin Slime raped me and had been for a while. He would beat my ass when I told him I would tell you guys," I lied.

I hoped Queen took my word for it. She and her cousin Slime had one thing in common. They were crazy about me, so I felt I could get away with anything. Until now, I watched in my rearview mirror as she pointed her gun at the back of my head.

"I love you, Queen. Don't do this," I begged as I pulled the car over to plead my case. Once I put the car in park, I climbed into the back seat. She had me fucked up right now. I wasn't going out by her hands.

"No, you don't. You used me." Queen wasn't lying. I did, but it happens.

I used one hand to lower her gun to the floor and used the other hand to pull her close to me. I kissed her lips softly, giving her pecks. Once I had her mind gone, I pulled her dress up. Attention was all Queen wanted. I used my hands to help her out of her thong while still kissing her gently. Her breathing got heavy on me. I sat back in my seat so she could access me fully. We undressed one another without disconnecting our lips. It wasn't like I was gay. Maybe I was curious.

Queen whispered, "If you would just stop chasing the niggas in my family. You would see I'm just as rich as they are. All you have to do is act right and let me love you."

That shit made me wet. I would probably take her up on that offer now that Prince wanted me dead. Queen was the closest thing to Prince. She was his weakness, and she was wrapped around my finger.

Chapter Ten

King Brown

"So, how are you going to do this shit now that Dexx is dead?" Blade asked.

I looked at him from the corner of my eye. I didn't acknowledge him, because I couldn't trust this nigga like I wanted to. Adapting to this life and how it operated took me a while. Just freely trusting niggas and bitches was out of the question. I'd been trying to get back right in the game, but I couldn't catch a break either way.

Blade was one of those niggas that spoke too much. He ran his mouth as bitches did, so I had to watch what I said around him. I wasn't even cool with the nigga being let in on the deal. Blade and Dexx had been handling our stash house in Jersey City. I didn't know much about him or how he worked. I met him months back when he came to me and told me about Peanut. I had to think about the shit.

My Uncle Peanut and cousin Slime were bad for business. I needed the business at the time, because shit was going all wrong on my end. I needed the money and bad. I had so much shit I needed to handle, including debts my ass got in that nobody but Dexx knew about. We had a different type of relationship. It was sad to see his outcome, but I wasn't about to tell on myself. Prince had done so much for me, my brother, and my sister. Since we'd been out, I ain't had to worry about nothing.

After a while, I started to feel like I was a burden. Family or not, I couldn't get used to being taken care of. I needed something

I could say I built. It was time I did my own thing for real. I needed to get out of Prince's hair and on my own feet. It may seem like I let my brothers down, but it was not like that. I was the only one that felt the family was family. Since I knew how these niggas worked, I let the bullshit go on. Everything was going smoothly until a nigga got too hungry.

I pulled my pre-rolled blunt from my ear, lit the fat end of it, and inhaled the smoke. I choked a little, which meant the weed was good. I pulled the blunt again, taking in the smoke through my nose and mouth and held it before letting the smoke out. A nigga was feeling the buzz, so I finally answered Blade's question. "I got this. Just play your position, and we're good."

I tried to make sure the nigga got the picture. He seemed scared, and scared niggas did too much to the point where I couldn't take them seriously. I started the car and cut my music up. I looked at the nigga Blade, so he'd get the clue and get out. Blade shook his head and opened the passenger side door. He let himself out and closed the door behind him.

I pulled off on his ass, spinning tires. I was somewhat mad as I glanced in my rearview mirror at him still standing there. I watched as a black car with tints pulled up to him. That was all I could make out. I stayed there, ensuring it was who I needed it to be. Two shots were fired, giving me the green light to go.

After watching Blade's body hit the ground, I pulled off with my mission accomplished. I laughed as I hit the highway. I had enough time to make my rounds and pick up my girl. She and her family had a family gathering after the loss of her dad.

I made my way back to my side of the town, slowing down soon as I hit the hood. The police were hot, and the last thing I needed was another ticket or to get locked up for the drugs on me, not to mention the nine-millimeter under my seat. I was throwing bricks at the jail with the way I was riding.

I was glad I slowed my ass down 'cause as soon as I hit the

corner store, the cops set up a roadblock. I bucked a U-turn and headed the back way. There was no need to check the spot out on that end. The trap would be slow for a few hours due to the roadblock. My mind raced after pulling off onto the highway and heading straight to my girl's house. I needed a drink to put some hair on a nigga's chest.

Knowing about it and being in on the shit was even more of a risk. I didn't think my uncle would go this far with the beef. He hated my dad and his dad so much. So, why would I want to do business with him? For one, their intentions weren't as bad as Prince thought they were. All they wanted was to get into business with us. I held one conversation with them, and they cleared the air for me. I was sure of two things: it wouldn't get back to me, and I wasn't in those videos Prince watched.

I had a thirty-minute drive to get to my girl, and I would be thinking about what I'd done the whole time. As always, pussy could get a nigga fucked up — good pussy at that.

I pulled up to my girl's family house and texted her to let her know I was there. Mandy came outside crying like she was when I dropped her off. She opened the door and sat down, wiping her eyes. Shawty was still emotional over losing her father, Dexx. In the last week, she'd lost her job and her dad's car. She had to clean his things out and put them in storage.

There was no way I could attend the gathering. I was the reason he was dead, so it didn't sit right with me being in his house. I felt the dude's spirit or ghost would follow my ass. Dexx knew he couldn't stop shit even if he wanted to. What a nigga like me wants, a nigga like me gets. He had to learn that shit the hard way, but now it's too late.

I met Mandy when I dropped Dexx off at her house. She had just come back from vacation with her mother and came out to the car to speak to him. From that day on, I'd been chasing after her ass.

The only problem we had was her being white. I wasn't ready for my niggas to clown me. When I first laid eyes on my snow bunny, she played like she didn't see a nigga checking her out. I guess that's what they call playing hard to get. I made it a point to take her punk-ass daddy home to see her every day.

Dexx had been working for us for a good two years. That's when I found out Lexx was his brother. I never told a soul. I wanted my brother to think I found this nigga on my own. He and I had just gotten out of prison. Dexx and his brother Lexx were in the mob. The connections he had helped me get back right. So, what nigga wouldn't use his resources to get rich?

After we changed the plans for the drop, I was the one to inform Dexx. He let Peanut and Slime know. Most of the work I did was in the background. I would rather be heard than seen.

"I missed you, ma," I told Mandy as I pulled her close to me.

"I miss my dad," she cried.

It hurt to see her upset or crying, so I rubbed her back to help soothe her. As I sat quietly on the driver's side, I wouldn't know how she'd react to the truth. I wanted to tell her what her dad and I were into, yet I wasn't slow. I loved her, but not to the point where I would snitch on myself. Mandy probably wouldn't believe what her dad did, anyway. In her eyes, he could do no wrong. He made everything look good as she grew up. She had a closed mind to the life we lived. That's why this was so hard for her.

"I wish I could get him back for you, baby," I told her, finally sympathizing with her.

I pulled into our yard. We had taken that big step and moved into a nice ass house nine months ago. That's where some of Prince's money was going. We talked about being married one day. That was how deep we were into one another.

Meanwhile, I couldn't tell a soul how happy I was with

Mandy. I wasn't embarrassed. It was just too much to handle.

I put the car in park and cut off my engine and headlights. Neither of us made a move. I was feeling her pain. Dexx was cool with me. He just fucked up and got caught on that camera. I started to say something to ease the mood but got interrupted by my phone. Mandy looked at me and jumped out. I began to go after her, but the text message I received fucked me up.

973-678-1393: I'm back in town, and I have somebody I want you to meet.

I knew the area code but not the number.

Me: Who the fuck is this?

It took four seconds for her name to come across my screen. I almost shitted myself. Man, this shit just kept getting crazier. I might have to leave town if this shit got out.

Yeah, a nigga was in a fucked-up spot. I'd done some dirt in my past, and it was all coming back to haunt me. How does somebody come back years later to pick up where they left off? That was the only question I had for her ass.

This bitch had been blackmailing me for years, and I couldn't say shit. So, when she texted me, I had no choice but to meet her. Makayla wasn't the average chick. Shawty was bad and smart. Yet, sometimes it's such a thing as being too intelligent. Shawty let her beauty and brains go to her head. My brother met shawty in high school before he and Kesha got serious. He met Kesha through Makayla when Makayla and Kesha were best friends.

They lived together, got their apartment at seventeen, and got their first job. Makayla started working with her dad at the doctor's office and put Kesha on. My brother came home from the doctor telling me he met two bad bitches that worked there and got both of their numbers. He told me he would talk to them both as long as he didn't get caught, but once Makayla gave up some ass, he stopped texting Kesha.

No lie. Makayla had my boy's nose wide open. She had him stealing cars, sticking up old ladies, and doing anything else he could do for money. Back in the day niggas wanted bruh's head for fucking with Makayla. When he found out she was fucking everything and everybody, and he started back texting Kesha.

I came along and started fucking Makayla right before they broke up. He was fucking with Kesha the long way, so I didn't think he would care. Besides, I was his brother, so I came before these hoes. The problem was that I got caught slipping more than once.

A few niggas confronted me over her, because she was out here letting all types of niggas hit it raw. I could look at these niggas and tell they had something, so why was Makayla fucking them?

We weren't even a couple, so I had to fall back from the hoe. I didn't need any other nigga thinking we were a thing. Around that time, Kesha and my brother came out with their relationship. All hell broke loose when they did. Kesha and my brother had been fucking behind her back. They were best friends, but once that aired out, Makayla wanted her head.

Makayla wasn't trying to let me go. She wanted me to come clean, but I told her ass I'd deny ever fucking with her. Who would my brother believe, a hoe or his blood? Plus, she got too comfortable, and I blamed myself. I gave her too much pull, and it backfired.

I did what any nigga in my position would have done. I gave her the money to move out of the state. After buying her ticket, I watched her ass leave two days later. It was sad to see her go, but I needed my life back. So, I lied and told her I would move there with her. It was the only way she'd go. I got the money off my brother and sent her ass on. I didn't mind doing it, because things were out of hand.

I told her she had to go and get a job before I came to be with her, but shortly after she left town, I got locked up. I couldn't catch a break for shit. Things were out of control, and I needed to fix them.

I put in the address to where I needed to go and headed out. I sent out a text, making sure everything was in place. I had two hours to get there and five hours until I had to be back. As soon as I hit the highway, my phone rang. I used the keypad on my dashboard to accept the call. The name came across too late. I would have declined the shit if I saw who it was before I answered, "Yeah?"

"What's up, nephew? You told your brothers about our little arrangement yet?" My punk-ass uncle asked, joking like shit was funny.

"Nawl, what's up with your boy, Blade? I ain't heard from him." I lied, knowing I just had that man hit the other day.

Peanut got silent, which had me smiling. Yeah nigga we're family as fuck. I was just as crazy as, or crazier than, he was. "You didn't?" he asked.

I disconnected the call and headed to meet the next problem I had to solve. At this point, anybody that had one over me had to go.

Chapter Eleven

Major

My mind couldn't rest for shit. Kesha had been in the hospital in the ICU for two weeks. Come to find out, she was six weeks pregnant and had lost our baby. A nigga was hurt and ready to kill whoever had my girl going through this shit. I remember when Kesha told me she was pregnant with my twins. It wasn't a surprise because I came from a family of twins. My brother King and I were twins. I was the happiest man alive, and nothing and no one could change that. Just to see my girl laying here like this hurt a nigga.

I ain't eat, sleep, or shit for days and wanted to leave here with her. I couldn't take seeing her like this. I chased after Makayla and got my girl hit. I had all types of thoughts going through my head, but none made any sense. I needed Kesha to pull through, because there was so much shit left for us to do. Getting married was now at the top of my list. My baby deserved my last name, and I wouldn't have it any other way. A nigga was scared if I closed my eyes, I'd miss her opening hers. I prayed like hell my baby would come through. I couldn't see my life without her in it.

I wiped my eyes, stood to my feet, and walked away from her bedside. She didn't need to see me crying if she woke up. I had to get myself together. I was losing it and fast. I didn't want to seem like a weak-ass nigga, but this shit had broken me. I walked to the window just to clear my mind and heard the hospital room door open.

In stepped Makayla and baby girl, and I wasn't sure how to

feel. The same two people I saved were the reasons my girl looked like this. No matter how hurt I felt, I couldn't front it like I wasn't glad Makayla stuck around to see if Kesha was okay. Showing she cared meant a lot to Kesha and me. I wanted to talk about the situation at hand.

Makayla probably wouldn't mind us getting a blood test, but I wasn't taking any chances. When she told me she was coming, I hollered at this nurse named Courtney to see what I could do and how I could do it. I was willing to pay a small price if it came to that. Like most bitches I encountered, the nurse wanted some dick for doing the shit, but a few bands sounded more reasonable to me.

"How is she? Has she woken up yet?" Makayla asked.

I only shook my head. I wasn't in the mood for words. I also wasn't trying to push Makayla away until I knew if Imani was my child. Baby girl came over and hugged me, making a nigga break down even more. I swear I needed that. I returned the hug a little longer to make up for the lost time. Once I let go, she returned to her mom with her head down. I wondered if she knew what had just happened. She was way too young to go through any of this. I guessed it was called being in the wrong place at the wrong time.

I walked back over to Kesha's bed and kissed her on the lips. I wanted to break down again, but too many eyes were on me. Once I kissed her, I headed out the door. I wasn't going far, just to the bathroom while waiting for the nurse to check on her. I needed a shower and some sleep, but now wasn't the time.

I also didn't fully trust Makayla by herself with my girl, because shit wasn't right. I wasn't sure what she came back on, but I peeped the hate in her eyes at my house. I could tell it hurt her to see my baby mama and I was still going strong. I, too, felt bad because I was fucking them both back then, but once Kesha and I took it there, it was a wrap.

Not saying I was a perfect angel, but Kesha made a nigga

change his ways. She slowed me down for my good, and then came my kids. They made a nigga think differently. For them, I couldn't go back to jail, so I watched how I moved. I also watched who I moved with.

Walking into the bathroom, I raced to the stool and didn't know how badly I had to go until I sat down. I was glad I was wearing sweatpants. It would have been over for me had I been wearing jeans. I relieved myself, washed my hands, and walked back toward Kesha's room.

My phone started ringing. Once I saw it was my twins' school, I picked it right up.

"Hello, is everything okay with my twins?" I asked, not even saying hello first. I got straight to the point of the call because I had already had enough on my plate.

"They are acting out. Please come have a chat with them." The teacher's assistant, who just so happened to be my ex, stated.

When a nigga first started fucking in middle school, she was my third victim. I did her and her sister at the same time, and she thought I would stick around. What the fuck did I look like when you offered me up to your family member? I wasn't the type to turn down pussy back then. I was still young and learning. Nowadays, I don't even look these hoes' way.

Part of me wanted to believe she was calling my kids out on some other shit because of what I put her through.

"Maybe it's because their mother had been in the hospital fighting for her life!" I barked, hanging up.

As I made my way back to Kesha's room, I walked right into the nurse who was about to help me with this blood test. Real shit, I knew Makayla and my brother had been fucking hard back then, and he just never said a word. I waited for the nigga to speak on it, but he didn't. I wondered why he didn't just come clean. I wasn't mad, but he could have told a nigga.

His secrecy made me wonder what the fuck else he was doing behind my back. King did me a favor by taking Makayla off my hands. Hell, he sent the bitch off, taking her off our hands. When Kesha and I got tight, she was my only focus. I let all these hoes go when she started having my kids.

"All I need you to do is get the mom out of the room for at least twenty minutes. Leave baby girl with me, and I'll get her blood work done," Courtney instructed.

I nodded, went on my mission, and walked into Kesha's room with the nurse. Imani was lying in the chair, sleeping next to her mother. I walked up next to Makayla and whispered in her ear. I knew what to say to make her leave her mind, body, and soul right then. Her eyes widened, and I stepped back and held out my hand as she took it and stood up.

We walked out, and I gave the nurse the okay to do her thing. Makayla didn't even look back to check on baby girl. She started holding my arm and shit, but I let her have her moment. I thought I was seeing shit 'cause I saw my girl open her eyes as we walked out. It was good and bad. I didn't want her to think anything of this. Kesha had a nigga's mind, body, and soul wide open out this bitch.

The only one that should be hurt was Makayla, because I wasn't about to let shawty suck this dick ever again. I planned to take her to my car and ask her just enough questions to make this time go by before I could return to my girl. Makayla would hate me when she figured out I only wanted to get her away from the room. I hoped the test would come back soon.

Once we reached my car, I let Makayla inside and started the engine. I cut my heat on. It was cold as fuck.

Shawty grabbed my belt as soon as she got comfortable in the seat.

"Chill, we got time, so tell me why you want to fuck me so

bad? What else did you come back for?" I asked.

That was an honest question. It was like Makayla was there to fuck something up. I needed to know just what that was, because there was a child involved. I didn't mind beefing with anybody. Just keep my family out of it.

"I'm not up to anything. Hell, I thought I was sucking some dick. That's all."

I didn't buy that for one minute. "So, where are you staying, and how long are you here for?" I asked, buying some time.

"Look, I don't know! Don't drill me this way. Drill me in another way," Makayla flirted as she put her hands in her tights and propped her leg up in my seat, playing with herself.

No lie, it was sexy to see, but that was all.

She pulled her fingers out and licked them hoes clean.

I just shook my head and closed my eyes, wondering why I put myself in this shit. I didn't make these types of mistakes, so I cut the car off and got out on her ass. Makayla yelled out behind me, but I didn't stop. She always did too much, and I wondered how many niggas she had done that with. It didn't matter. All of this would soon be over or just starting.

Before returning to my girl's room, I went to the restroom to wash my face. I did wanna know if she was up or if I was seeing shit. I dried my eyes and face with paper towels and left the bathroom. As soon as I hit the hallway, Makayla walked into Kesha's room, smiling hard. I walked in, and Kesha was up with the nurse and baby girl. I raced to her side, but she gave me a cold look when I reached her, letting me know she saw ole girl and me leaving together.

"Don't even come over here. You've been missing in action with your other baby mama," Kesha spewed with tears in her eyes.

She had a nigga ready to cry. Little did she know, we did

nothing.

Makayla had to say something. "Yup, boo, you got to share that dick like I had to!"

"Ain't shit like that going on, Makayla. Don't lie. I just curved that loose pussy, ma," I gritted. She had me fucked up for acting like we were doing something.

The noise started escalating to where the nurse had to shush us.

"Just leave all of you!" Kesha ordered.

I looked around, trying to understand who the fuck she was talking to. I wasn't going anywhere without her. "I know you think you know some shit, but you don't, so I'll let you cool off. I love you, and I'll be back later."

I walked over to kiss Kesha, but she moved her head to the other side. I just let that be and walked off. Makayla and baby girl had already left. I was glad she was gone, because she did too much.

"I got the test done, so when the results are in, I will call you." Courtney informed me when I walked out of the room.

I reached into my pocket and pulled off some money to give her. She waved me off and walked away. I guessed it was on her. I got outside to my car and headed to my grown-ass twin's school. So much for my ass getting some rest since they were acting out.

∞∞∞

"Promise and Passion, why am I not surprised that it's you two distracting my class?"

I should have walked in there to stop my girls from acting out, but I did not. I needed to hear what these two had been up to.

Kids act out in school when something isn't going right at home. So, in my eyes, I was seeing if that theory was true or not. The closer I got to the class, the more I heard my girls cutting up.

"Since you're not surprised, why did you call us out?" Passion said.

My mouth dropped. Everyone laughed out loud like they were funny or something. I fucked around and started laughing out loud, too. I took my laugh to the extreme, because when the fuck did my girls start acting like this, and why am I just now being told?

"Since they are so funny to you all, how about everybody laughing can join them in detention," the teacher said, followed by a crazy laugh.

"Write it up, teach. They down with us." Promise boasted as the class laughed aloud again.

I looked through the window, and these damn girls were sitting at their desks, dressed in clothes I didn't see their ass leave in this morning. I see why I got that call. The kids were going off. One tall ass little boy sat down next to my baby, so I walked into the class and let my presence be known.

My daughters knew better than this type of behavior. I was sure their mother being hurt brought this on. We didn't live like this, and their mother would flip her wig. They were only ten, about to be eleven, and already showing out. I hoped to God this was only because their mama was sick, and that was the only reason they were acting out.

"Daddy!" Promise yelled, jumping down off the desk.

Passion didn't move. She had a stinking look on her face, like I was bothering her ass.

"What y'all asses got going on? Get off the desk, Passion." I could not believe I had to tell her little ass that from the get-go.

"Why are you here, daddy?" Passion asked, like she was a little off or something. Even Promise gave her the neck break look, like, *what the fuck you mean, sis?*

I couldn't help but laugh as I pulled them both out the classroom door. I grabbed their asses by the arm and damn near yanked them out.

"Why am I here, you asked. Hahahaaa." I laughed. I smacked my hand on my leg, carrying on with my laughing. I didn't give a fuck about this school or lesson. These kids had to be taught a real-life lesson.

I was there for one reason: to get this point across to them. I laughed so hard that I fell on the floor, kicking my long legs out, trying to embarrass them. I had the kids in the class laughing and the kids in the hallway. Even the teacher came and looked on in amazement. I was doing what they just did, but it backfired on them. There was no worse punishment than to have your parents come to the school and act like the clown you were pretending to be.

I got up, fixed my clothes, and kissed them both on the forehead. "If you don't want me to come back up here and embarrass you again, you better act like you have some sense in that class. Keep on, and everyone will think you're crazy like your daddy." I walked off laughing. I did what I needed to. My job was done, and they were ashamed. I could tell they wanted to leave with me but nope.

As I knocked on the door to go, my ex came into the hallway, smiling. I did not even look her way. I was in enough trouble as it was with my girl over a bitch, so I kept it moving. I needed to holla at Prince to see if he heard from King's ass.

Chapter Twelve

Prince

"Thank you for taking the time out to see me today," Lexx said, greeting me.

I stepped in and sat at the round table he had in front of me. I nodded and waited for what this meeting was about. It was a last-minute meeting, and I started not to come. From the looks of me being the only one here, I shouldn't have come.

"I know you're wondering why I called you here and alone. I wanted to take this time to show you one of your team players. From the footage I've captured, I wouldn't say they were being a team player," Lexx explained as he started the video for me.

I sat back and watched my flesh and blood betray me. In front of my very eyes, to say the least. As I watched the person in the footage exchange handshakes and take a big black bag, I was pissed. I wanted to know what the fuck was in that shit.

My prayers were answered when the video showed the person pulling out the same guns Lexx gifted us. Everything was stolen the day the person in this footage ran me off the road. Everything was now making sense to me, and I needed to know just how I would play this.

"I'll take it over from here, Mr. Lexx. Thank you for putting a nigga up on game. I won't even ask how you got this shit," I joked as I shook his hand to leave.

"I can't tell you my secrets. I'd have to kill you. You have too much work here on these streets, so let's skip that chat," he replied.

I just smiled and found my way out of Lexx's office. Part of me wanted to be mad that I came out all this way just to find out this information. He could have sent a nigga a few pictures.

I guess my not wanting to leave Chime played a big part in my acting like this. Shawty had a hold on me, and I didn't care. I was comfortable with whatever hold Chime had on a nigga. It felt good to me. A nigga felt soft and warm inside with the mention of her name. The sight of her face made me weak, which was more of why I knew I needed to fall back. I didn't want either of us to get hurt. One thing a nigga like me wasn't was a fuck boy. I don't play games. I'm upfront with bitches from the gate.

I let them know what I'm looking for, and most of the time, it was only head. Bitches didn't know how to handle good dick and go on about life. There were always either feelings or money involved, and I was sick of females that didn't know what they wanted. I also know Lyric was still acting like her shoe size, so I stuck to what was familiar to keep the peace.

I boarded the plane back to Louisiana, taking my seat at the window as I had done on the way here. I couldn't sit by the aisle. It made a nigga feel some type of way. I also had to sit close to the back, but not too close to the bathroom, 'cause that motherfucker be stinking. I couldn't eat, sleep, or even focus around something that smelled like ass. I have always been big on hygiene.

My phone beeping interrupted my thoughts, letting me know I got a message. I saw it was from Chime, letting me know she missed me. A nigga sent her a text asking her how much. Within seconds, my phone alerted me that I had picture mail.

I was hoping it was an ass picture, but her being a virgin, I was sure all she sent a nigga was a picture of her smiling and shit.

When I read her message, I got the shock of my life. Chime had a nigga ready to fly this bitch just to hurry and get back to her ass. Yeah, I can see how she enjoys playing these little games. I bet after I put this dick in her life, she won't be playing anymore.

I took a picture of my dick on soft, and I didn't give a fuck about who was around me. If their eyes saw through my travel blanket, they needed to see this dick. I sent off my picture and cut my phone completely off. I wasn't one for going back and forth. Chime just needed to get that pussy ready 'cause a nigga was ready to fuck.

∞∞∞

I had to make this last stop like I promised Lyric's godmother. I wanted to leave her some money to help her out with Harmony. I knocked on the door, and seconds later, Harmony came to the door.

"Why are you back here?" She asked and started to close the door. I had to stop it with my feet without scaring her.

"I'm looking for Grams this time, lil' mama," I informed her.

Little mama stared me up and down. She had a nigga feeling real short. Knowing I stood every bit of six-foot-two, I couldn't help but laugh. I was looking at a split image of Lyric and Slime. I had Grams blood test little mama, and she wasn't my daughter. It was cool. I was the type of nigga to still take care of her family.

"Move on out of the way, Harmony! Prince wants to be your godfather, honey. Now be nice," I heard Grams say.

"How is it going today for you?" she asked.

I pulled an envelope out of my back pocket and handed it to her. She pulled me into the house and fixed me a plate.

I stayed and got to know Lyric's Grams, Ms. Mable. She was wise and kind, and I hated learning how sick she was as she cared for Harmony. It was bad enough that she was already in a wheelchair, but she also was a diabetic. I needed to know how Lyric ended up having Ms. Mable take care of Harmony.

After talking for hours with Ms. Mable, she told me everything about Lyric. She also informed me that Lyric had popped up at the church one day, taking her home with her. Come to find out, Lyric was kidnapped as a child.

∞∞∞

Five hours later, I left Ms. Mable's house and headed to the address she had for Lyric with my brothers. I had my niggas check the spot before we even left Ms. Mable's place. I couldn't break the news to her about her godchild as I wanted to. Harmony didn't deserve to hear the type of mother she had. Little mama is an angry child, and I couldn't even blame her. Hell, she was just as lost as I was when it came to her mother. I didn't even know who Lyric was anymore. I couldn't even say I loved her. I had strong feelings at one point, but time changed that.

We waited up the street out of the way of the address I was giving. After staking out the house for three hours, nothing seemed out of the ordinary. As soon as the thought left my mind, out walks Lyric walking hand in hand with Slime. It took everything in me not to shoot at them both.

Timing was everything, which meant they would get theirs in due time. I never tripped off anybody doing me wrong because karma was a motherfucker. My niggas and I were posted watching Slime, Peanut, and Lyric chop it up. Rule number one is to always be very aware of your surroundings. That's the code in the hood, to be real, so these niggas were tripping. A nigga like me didn't underestimate anybody. My own family has been switching up on me for years.

We waited a long while before leaving the car. Once we

reached the backyard, Major started pouring out gasoline. King popped the lock to the back door, and we made ourselves at home. I was hoping everybody in this bitch was asleep.

After we poured gasoline everywhere around the house, we all made our exit. Before I lit the match, I waited long enough for my crew to get far away from the house. I sat back and watched the flames take over half the place before we all left. Once I was pleased, we hit the highway and made our way home.

Three down, one to go. That meant my very own brother King. It was time to holla at Chime to put forward my next move. From the way this nigga been looking at Chime, I was sure she was his next move. A nigga like me was ready for whatever, though. Chime was going to have to play this game my way for me.

Chapter Thirteen

Makayla Owen

I couldn't lie with a straight face if I wanted to. Things were finally working for the good. I had Major and Kesha's no-good asses right where I needed them. Kesha and I had some unfinished business to handle, and I couldn't wait. I was done living this double-ass life, and they all had to pay.

Kesha would pay first since she was the one that took my man from me. It was not like I was hurt, just more disappointed in how I let it get to me. It's called trust and loyalty. You were never supposed to fuck a nigga behind your best friend, or any friend, for that matter. That hoe forgot the girl code.

I didn't know how to feel when I found out about them. I was too busy fucking around with King to care what she had going on. Still, everything I went through from that day on was because of this family. I wanted my get-back and money out of the deal — if I were lucky, I would kill Kesha. I was back to do more than collect from them 'cause they all had me fucked up.

I wanted to start by being sweet to Kesha to see if we had anything left. Yet, the moment she pissed me off, wanting to fight over a man she took from me, it was on. Now I planned to get her out of the way and for good, even if that meant being a stepmom to her kids while their daddy and I made some of our own.

I only mentioned my daughter being Major's kid, but on the real, I had four kids, and two belong to the family. Major just wasn't the father. King was the father of my son and my daughter, and he didn't even know it. I felt better off saying my daughter belonged to Major because he had two daughters that he took good care of.

Major was more on his shit. Plus, between him and his brother, Kesha lucked up for real. King wasn't at all a bad catch. He was just a bum-ass nigga compared to Major. I tried my best to shape and mold his ass, but he ended up flexing on me. I put that nigga on game, changed his ways and style, and kept money in his pocket.

Most would say I was a bitch that would buy a nigga, but it was nothing like it. I did what any bitch would do who was holding her man down. At the end of the day, Major was done with me after discovering all the niggas I fucked. He needed to understand that was all I was used to. This shit was all just a game at first, but then I caught feelings and only cared for him. I used other guys to get what we needed.

At first, things were great. I was head over heels for Major's ass. I could say he felt the same way. He did something for and to me that no other man would. Still, I hadn't had a man to fuck me and eat me as well as he did. King was good in bed but needed to grow up, because he wasn't eating ass yet.

King was a good five-foot-nine two hundred pounds flat. He was sexy like his brothers. They all had that sexy brown skin complexion. His dreads were to his shoulders but real thin. He kept up with them, so he was cool. He also had a goatee, but it was for nothing.

I wasn't a bad look myself. I had light skin with light brown eyes, chink eyes, and my lips were full. My body was to die for. Who would have thought I would still be a bad bitch after four kids? I was much older now, and I had too much to lose. Therefore, I had to watch how I did things. I wasn't happy-go-lucky as they thought I was back in the day.

How would you feel if your own fucking best friend took your man? Everyone wanted to make me out to be the bad guy.

The only reason anyone was mad was that I was playing niggas, doing to them what they did to us. The funny part was, so was my best bitch. We were known to get a nigga and tag team his ass, but Kesha kept that part out when she met Major. We knew he was texting us both. We were best friends, which meant we told one another everything.

We stayed together and made our licks together, so most of our house was on camera. The night she fucked Major, she got the kind of sex I'd been chasing him for. There I was years later, still mad they did me that way. I wanted in if anything, but Major moved Kesha out shortly after she got that dick.

I hated going back in time like I was into a lot of shit. I knew that one day it would all come back to bite me. I just waited on when.

While my daughter slept, I stepped out of the hotel for a little while. I went to three stores to get something to eat and clothes to wear. I was running out of cash, so I was back in town to see how they came up. I wanted what I should have had back then. If not, I'd take it.

Making it back to my room, I knew my daughter was up, but she knew how to work her tablet and the television. I grabbed all the bags and used my foot to close my door. Once I reached the lobby, I headed to the side door. I got one of the pushcarts to help me get all this shit to the room. I got caught off guard by all the police officers in the lobby. I pushed the up button for the elevator door, still looking around.

It almost felt like I was being watched or they were waiting on me. Damn, I should have hit that line. A bitch was tripping hard once the elevator came, and I got on. Two officers jumped on as soon as the door was getting ready to close. *Why did they wait until the last minute to get on? Were they looking for somebody on my floor?*

I asked, "What floor?"

They looked and laughed at one another. "You caught us. It's you we're looking for. I'm Officer Davis, and this is Officer Dick. Can we ask you a few questions about last night?" The chubby one asked. He was all in my face.

"Okay, yeah."

"Do you know who shot Kesha or at you and your daughter?" The skinny police officer asked.

I was glad it was time to get off. This was starting to feel weird as fuck. I had been gone for years, so I was just getting back in town, and that was what they needed to understand. "I didn't see anything. Had I done it, you all would have known." I snapped, getting off and walking to my room.

"Do you know why anyone would want to hurt you guys?" the fat fuck asked.

I just gave him a bothered look. I reached my room and heard my daughter moving around. "I'm just getting in town, so no, I don't know anything or anyone who wants to kill me."

I hated cops, so in my mind, I had already said too much. I had to watch the way I spoke to them, though. I wasn't trying to piss them off to get a bad name with the cops.

"Okay, well, if that was all, I have to get my family ready to eat," I said, hoping they got the clue. I didn't need them or their help. What I was into had already put my life in danger.

I set up that shooting. I had an old friend come to the address I gave him. It was no secret that I wanted Kesha out of the way and fast. She was the only person standing in my new family's way. I wanted her life, her man, and his money, and I was going to get it. I didn't care if she knew I had something to do with it. She had to see me one way or another.

It took no time to find out where Major and Kesha stayed. Social media is a bitch. When I found out they were happy as hell playing house in a beautiful ass condominium, all I could think was that she owed me. I was in town to collect every single dime, too.

I was what you called salty as hell. I could have had a better life had she not changed up. So, it was my pleasure to get my boy to shoot at the house. I was mad we were out there when it happened. That was too close for my liking. I was angry when I figured out she was still alive, and he almost hit my ass. I had to finish the job, and my dear friend wouldn't get all the money we discussed because Kesha was still breathing.

I went to the hospital for two reasons: to show my face and end her life. But as always, things didn't work out like I wanted, outside of being tricked into leaving the room. I felt I was getting closer. I thought I was hearing shit when Major whispered in my ear. Real shit, he didn't even have to ask. I would suck his dick through a straw if he needed me to. I jumped up so fast that I barely gave him a chance to ask the entire question. I headed to the door before Major could finish his sentence, and it was then that I saw Kesha open her eyes. I wanted her to see me leading her man out the door. Payback was a bitch named Makayla. I couldn't wait to slide that dick down this throat and make him stay.

It was too good to be true, though. I believed Major wanted to but felt bad. The bitch was half dead in the hospital bed, so he couldn't have chosen a better time and place. I wasn't as mad as he thought. I was on to my next mission. Once shit got ugly, I left out that bitch flying. I'm glad Kesha and Major were beefing. It was time to play this game the way I'd wanted to play it the last few years. I was back and had something for them all.

I waited until the cops were out of sight. I needed to start packing up my shit since it was that easy to find me for them. I was in the wrong place. Maybe it was best to skip a few towns to keep my daughter out of the way.

"Hey, mommy, guess what? The guy you said is my other

daddy came by soon as you left," my daughter said, coming out of the bathroom.

I peeped out the window, checking the parking lot and making sure nobody followed me or that the cops hadn't doubled back. I have been there and had that happened to me, which is why I was checking out this hotel.

"Why did you let him in, honey?" I hoped she was speaking of Major. I didn't need King knowing my whereabouts just yet.

I grabbed all I needed and stuffed it in our bags, ensuring nothing important was left. I got my charger from the wall, packed my daughter's iPad, and headed for the bathroom.

"Oh no, mommy, I didn't. I woke up, and he was sitting in the chair watching me. Oh yes, he left food and this paper beside my iPad."

Imani skipped over to pick up the paper next to her iPad. She handed me the paper, running as if it would disappear before reaching me.

I took the paper from her hand and stared down at it. I wanted to shit my pants at the writing and what it said. It was a little too late to be this up in the game. I thought I'd been getting over Major, but he knew everything. I looked down at the paper and read it aloud to ensure I read it right. This nigga somehow got my daughter's blood to take a blood test, and I knew nothing about it.

I packed all our shit and left the room, flying. As soon as we got inside the car, I buckled myself and started to take off. That's when I heard a gun click.

"So, when you want to talk about why you really here, and why you're fucking my brother, uncle, and a few other niggas around the way?"

I closed my eyes, hoping like hell this nigga didn't kill my ass.

Chapter Fourteen

Chime

"So, bae, remember what to do if he follows behind you. Be cool. Don't even be scared. I'm not gone let shit happen to you." Prince told me after giving me the rundown of how this party shit might go. I didn't know what it was about him, but I was all in.

"Ok, baby, I got it," I simply replied.

I had mixed emotions when it came to Prince. One second, I was ready to go home and get away from him. The next, I wanted him to show me why my body craved him so much. My feelings were all over the place, and I couldn't understand why. This man was not what I was used to, but every part of me wanted to be a part of his world. I felt like a kid back in high school.

It appeared Prince was a businessman and a gangster all in one. He acted a certain way when he was conducting business. I rode and attended a few meetings, because I was handling his money transactions. The way niggas gave him full attention when he stepped into a room was sexy. It didn't make it any better that he could dress his ass off.

I was glad Lyric wasn't around to take the picture when I drooled again from staring at him. She was no longer keeping it warm or playing her part. Not only did I look good, but I also felt good. My hair and makeup were slayed to the gods thanks to myself and Queen. I looked good, but Prince still was keeping me from my family and having me work all day.

"I need a break. I have to get out and have fun, like drinking and smoking. I need to do something before I go crazy." I expressed to Prince.

He smiled, walked over to me, placed my chin in the palm of his hand, and kissed me on my forehead. You see, this was the kind of shit I didn't get. It was like Prince loved confusing me. He held me captive yet kissed me like I was his treasure.

"We can hit one of my clubs later tonight, ma, okay? Don't be in a rush to show off my goodies. Shit, a nigga had to get you alone to bring this here look out of you," Prince replied.

Prince brought me out of the shell I was in. Not only did he move me into his house, but he also had a makeup station set up. I was happy and sad all in one because these were moments I wanted to share with my family. They were probably going crazy not hearing from me. I missed them too.

I didn't mind working for Prince, but he had to let me see my family sometimes. I was grateful he let me stay alive, even though I wasn't the one that stole from him. It showed he cared. I saw him in action these last few weeks, and he was capable of much worse. Yet, with me, he wasn't hardcore. Prince was gentle and calm but didn't know how to relax when we were around.

I needed to be around him to make my day complete. Never in my life had I felt like this. I knew Prince was into me before I changed my hair and clothes. That just made him even more protective of me. He said he needed to watch these niggas now that I came out of my shell. I was in love with the new me and couldn't wait to start on this new adventure. I couldn't believe how good I looked in the mirror these days.

If my grandmother were alive, she would be so proud. I had my hair pressed, wrapped, and color added to the tips. Queen talked me into trying blonde, which was a big step. I felt like I was jumping the gun, because I had never been the one to try new styles or colors. I left it to my twin sister to have bright colors and wild hairstyles. I loved how it showed Chance's boldness and wished I'd had it years ago.

"I guess it will do since I can't pick where I want to go," I told Prince, making sure he felt that shot was for him.

He kissed my lips and tapped me on the ass before walking out and leaving me to my thoughts and his actions. I was lost and sick of whatever he and I were doing. I was ready to be something more in his life, but I couldn't say a word to him about how I felt because of the position I was in. Since working for him, I had to tag along like a third wheel everywhere he went.

After being under his watch and care for a month, I was glad we were finally going out. I didn't care where to. Prince told me last week that if I made him two hundred and fifty grand, I could do what I wanted for a day. I had to bring it up again this week to make him stay true to his word. At the end of the day, I couldn't wait to get off and get dressed. It was time to find the right outfit for this outing, which meant hitting Queen up for help.

I sent Queen a text telling her I needed her help with an outfit. I kept her at a distance, because she and I never saw eye to eye until now. Don't let me leave out that she's the best friend of my enemy.

Nevertheless, I believed Queen and Lyric had a little more going on than being friends. I'd hoped I was wrong, but you could tell Queen was into girls. She let it be known every day on Facebook. Not only that, but I also heard rumors that Queen and Lyric had a train run on them. I wasn't sure if Prince knew or even cared, but in my eyes, that was too close for comfort. I didn't care to know much about them or their love life. They were just too much for me.

Prince left the office to get Mrs. Naomi, the chef, to prepare our lunch. We had been piled up with paperwork on the new property we were getting since nine o'clock this morning. I was past ready to eat and for my next break. This week I will receive my first bonus from him. Prince and his brother offered me a permanent position, and I took it. It was only under one condition. I had to stay in one of his spots. It sounded too good to be true, but he wanted to keep an eye on me to make sure I didn't go to the police or anybody else.

If Prince went down, I went down too. I was taking these folks' money, so who the fuck was I going to tell? After taking a deep breath, I let the rest of the day roll on. I wasn't sure how it would roll, but I was ready.

I headed to the bathroom, and my cell phone rang. It was unusual because my sisters were at work. I had already spoken to them both. I did not have any friends, so nobody called me. The number was also blocked. I opened the phone and answered it.

"Chime speaking, who's calling?"

"It's me, Queen. I dropped my phone in some water five minutes ago. I got your number from my brother. Sorry to call private, but I'm going to the new Gucci outlet. You want to go?" she asked.

"Absolutely," I said.

"Great, I'll be there in an hour. Let me handle my brother," she said and hung up.

∞∞∞

"Hold on, ma, where are you going in such a hurry, beautiful? Damn, you're so fine! I had to get close up on that ass to see you better!" Some dude hollered. He had been following us for the last four stores.

"Leave her alone. You know, that's Chime, one of the twins." Queen said to the dude.

He looked like this guy I had a class with in high school, but he got locked up the last time I heard. If this was Tay, he had upgraded his looks, too. He went from Steve to Stephan, like on the sitcom *Family Matters*.

"Shidddd, Chime. I used to have the biggest crush on her ass, but that nigga Prince always cock blocked on my ass. Fuck you doing hanging with her now, Queen?" Tay laughed as his crew came out of the Gucci store with both hands full of bags.

I could tell what type of shit they were into from all the gold chains and name-brand clothes. Hell, I could smell the loud from a mile away. Tay was so caught up in him telling me why Lyric and my sister had stopped being friends. Queen brushed the shit off, not wanting to get into it, but the Tay I remembered was a shit starter. He had just started his comedy hour, but I wasn't paying for the show. I walked off in the direction of the food court area, not trying to be rude, but I felt out of place. I made sure I sent Prince a text letting him know I missed him.

After ten minutes of me waiting on Queen, she shows up with Lyric's right-hand woman, Kim. She gave me a funny look the second she joined me with Queen. I returned the stare because a bitch like me was never scared.

For one, these people were not my family or friends, so I could not be comfortable around them. It seemed fake to be hanging with the crew of the same girl that had humiliated me on Facebook. I could not help but feel like I was being set up.

I wasn't at all scared, just aware that I didn't trust these hoes. Hearing my stomach growl, I needed to put something on my stomach. We left before I was able to eat the food the chef prepared. I had a few dollars on me, and it was enough to buy my food and drink.

Heading towards the restaurant, I looked back and Queen and Kim were right behind me. "Hey, wait for us, girl. A bitch is trying to get some tonight," Queen joked.

"Why are we even hanging with this bitch is the question? Lyric would kill us. This seems fake as hell, and I don't like it," Kim mentioned the same thing I was thinking. The problem was I didn't know she was coming.

I started to say something but chose not to. I'm just glad Prince gave me my phone to call him if I needed him while I was out, so I sent my sisters a text, letting them know where I was if anything went down.

Kim must have hit a nerve, because Queen snapped.

"Chill out! You didn't have to be here. I didn't ask you to come. I told you my brother is fucking with Chime, which means lay off her!" Queen finished as soon as the server approached us.

"Table for two or three?" The server interrupted Queen's outburst, trying to be funny.

I rolled my eyes as Queen got her straight. We followed behind the lady and sat close to a bar, which I was glad of. Seconds later, the bartender took our drink orders. I excused myself and went to the bathroom to text Prince to see what he was doing. I had been texting him the whole afternoon. I guess you could say I missed him a little.

When I reached the bathroom, he sent me a picture through picture mail. I smiled 'cause this man was full of surprises, so there was no telling what he sent. Hell, the only thing I asked him was what he was doing.

I opened the message and covered my mouth with my hand. It was a picture of Prince's big and juicy-looking manhood. This wasn't the first time he got me like this. He was out loud with this. He told me every day he wanted me but would wait until I was ready. Well, I was more than ready and willing. I just wanted the time to be perfect.

Under the picture, Prince wrote, *beating my dick until you stop playing with a nigga.*

I shook my head at my phone, because I was in the zone. I had never felt this way and didn't care how wrong it was. As long as he was single and I was single, we could do whatever without strings attached.

"His dick is big as hell, huh? And the nigga can fuck, but you'll never find that out. Yeah, Lyric is going to kill you." Kim sassed.

I was lost as to why Kim was madder than her friend was about the shit. Lyric knew her role these days, and I couldn't wait for her to come out of hiding. But until then, I was going to take this anger out on her bestie.

As much as I wanted to kick this hoe in the head and keep it moving, I knew I had to beat this bitch's ass like she stole something from me.

"Obviously you want this smoke since ya crazy ass followed me in here?" I wasn't too much on talking. I was more of the action type. These hoes weren't about to punk me back then or now.

"Yeah, I might." The bitch had the audacity to say.

I took off my jacket and put my hands in the air, trying to see what was up. Even though Lyric wasn't here, Kim wanted to play tough for her friend. It was sad to say she was about to catch these hands in every way. I was pissed and wanted to fight. At this point, the entire restaurant could get it.

I see why her brother told me to text him if anything weird jumped off. I wouldn't lie to Prince. These hoes wanted my head. When I texted him and told him Lyric's friend was with us, he assured me they wouldn't try anything, because they would have to deal with him. Well, this bitch was on one.

"Oh, bitch you're bold, huh?" Kim asked, coming right for me.

Before Kim could say another word, I ran up and kicked her

right in the chest, making her body fly back. I zoned out and started swinging nonstop. I pulled Kim by her hair and flung her around. Once her body hit the floor, I grabbed her by her hair and went to work, punching the bitch all in her face, chest, and head.

All I could think of was my life coming up with Lyric and her crew in high school. I hit her ass again, knocking a few of her teeth out.

"Bitch! Get up, hoe!" I yelled.

In one swift move out of nowhere, Prince yanked my ass up off her and headed for his car. As we walked by, I motioned for Queen to save me, but she shook her head no. She knew her brother was crazy, and I guess I was about to find out how crazy his ass was.

"Follow behind me, Queen! Hurry the fuck up! Y'all got shit looking hot!" Prince snapped at us like I had done something wrong.

Before we could make it to the car, Kim was following us. "You about to leave with this bitch for real, Prince? I can't wait to tell Lyric how you doing her."

Prince turned around and frowned. "Did you forget your homegirl set a nigga up bitch? You're lucky you're still breathing. How about you worry about that child you got by your cousin out here and get off my dick?" He gritted.

Prince must have hit a deep nerve. Kim pulled her phone out, took a picture, and dipped the fuck off. Out of nowhere, Prince took out his gun and shots were fired. I was glad Kim got out of the way. She was about to get fucked up again.

We got into Prince Benz and followed behind Queen. We were a good hour away from Prince's house, and I was ready to lay it down.

∞∞∞

We made it back to the house, and all I could do was shut my mouth, because I knew Prince was mad at me. He walked into the house and didn't say a word to me. I followed behind him like a sad dog. I hated this feeling.

"Fix your face. You got what you wanted out of your system. Now it's my turn, so let go, and I'm not playing," he snapped.

I made my way to the bathroom, ignoring his ass for real. I now had the attitude he had when he walked in. I started my shower, pulled all my clothes off, and jumped in. Prince wasn't about to let me live this one down, so I waited for him to come to join me, which he never did.

After I was dried off and fully dressed, I went to his master bedroom. I laid down, closed my eyes for a second, and ended up drifting off.

∞∞∞

Later that night, I completely changed my mind about going out. I had just gotten out of the shower again. Prince had Mrs. Naomi cook my favorite dish of stuffed chicken and pasta shells, and she did her thing. I eyed everything as he uncovered each entrée down to dessert. I was ready to eat everything from the salad to the corn on the cob.

I pulled the food next to me on the table in the master bedroom and started on the salad as Prince headed for the door.

"Where are you going? Are you not eating with me? What about the movie we were supposed to watch?" I questioned.

I was getting heated with all the running in and out shit he was doing. It was like he could no longer sit still around me anymore. He had something on his mind but wouldn't speak about it, so I took it there for him.

"Like, what am I doing wrong? Why don't you want me?" I added.

The look Prince gave me told it all. He closed the door and locked it, making his way over to me, and moving the food away from me before picking me up. I wrapped my arms around his neck and engaged him in a kiss while wrapping my legs around his waist. My juices were flowing as my breathing got heavy. I wasn't sure about this feeling, but I wanted to feel it. I couldn't believe how badly I wanted him and wanted it to be special.

Once we broke away, I pulled my clothes off one by one until I was completely naked. Prince licked his lips and looked at me with so much lust that it turned me on. I made him watch me as I played with my pearls. He was turned on. His manhood was now standing at attention through his pants, but he was taking too long.

I pulled him onto the bed with me and laid in the middle. There were no more words to be said. He knew what I wanted and needed. I may have been new to this, but trust me, I was going to show Prince a thing or two about how I felt. He pulled his shirt off and unbuckled his jeans. His clothes hit the floor fast.

I placed three fingers inside me, something I did before to get pleasure. My head rested on the pillow as I went to work. He could play all he wanted. I had toys, so I knew how to please myself.

"See, let your man handle this from here on out," Prince whispered in my ear.

My legs were spread apart in the air in one swift move. I then felt something wet and amazing on my pearl. I opened my eyes to see Prince eating my pussy and looking at me.

"Shitttt! Yes, bae, damn!" I moved my hips from left to right, following his motion.

"Can daddy have all of you tonight, ma?"

As if on cue, I busted in his mouth. He ate that shit until it made more water as he licked and sucked on my woman in the boat.

"Yes, I'm yours. I promise." I let out another one on his face.

Prince licked his lips and went to work. I then felt two fingers. I sighed as he played with my pearl while still eating and sucking. After a good twenty minutes of him pleasing me, he climbed on top of me and slid his thick, smooth dick into me. I damn near came clean off the bed, because it hurt so bad, but thankfully the pain eased up.

"I'm taking my time. Just let me in, ma."

I couldn't tell Prince was taking his time, but it didn't matter. My pussy was so wet and juicy that I matched his sexual pace as he rammed in and out of me. I let out all types of sounds. It felt so good that I couldn't even lie.

"Damn, that pussy tight, ma. What are you doing with this good ass pussy, ma?" He asked as he began speeding up the pace.

I could not keep up. Prince was on it. I gave him the best I had while he worked me over. Somehow, I ended up on top, which was all she wrote. I could feel him in my guts. It hurt and felt good all in one. I rode him slowly, getting my pussy ready for his full size. It felt better when I took control. When I felt comfortable, I started riding him like a cowgirl. I fucked around, tucked my hands under his head, and rode him to town. I watched as Prince's eyes rolled to the back of his head.

"Shit, I'm about to come, ma. Boot up!" he growled. Prince tossed me off of him and positioned me on my knees. He slid in from the back and started hitting it.

"Oh my God! Baby, yesss!" I let out as he hit it twice as hard. My moans and Prince smacking my ass were all that could be heard.

"Come with me, Chime," he ordered, but it was too late. I had released ten seconds ago. I felt his cum all in me as we fell onto the bed.

Prince looked me in the eye and shook his head before kissing me. "You know you mine now, right?"

My ass didn't answer. My mind drifted off to process what had just happened. I just fucked Prince and let him nut in me.

Chapter Fifteen

Prince

    I did not plan to give shawty this dick until shit calmed down with Lyric, but Chime had me fucked up in both heads. I had wanted her too bad for the last seven years. Chime wasn't a bitch off the street. She was my soul mate, and I knew that in high school. So, when those words left her lips, I had to make her eat them. Little did she know, what we just shared wasn't sex. We made love. I wasn't out here fucking bitches like it was cute or something to do. I wasn't the type of nigga to play games with her. I wanted what I wanted, so our souls tied once she got the dick.

    I have respect for women but seldom have more respect for them than they have for me. I had been in three genuine relationships. I was young but mature. The women I fucked with were older. Even Lyric was two years older than me. In my eyes, she was too young but not Chime. She was just right for a nigga. When we were young, I couldn't wait to feel our connection. I never said a thing to her because it wasn't the time or place. I wasn't ready for her back then.

    I didn't want to move too fast now that I had her. Chime knew exactly how I felt, so the ball was in her court. I just hoped she was prepared for a nigga like me. In due time, I would be able to tell, but for now, I have to stay focused. I had big shit going on out in these streets.

    For the last thirty days, niggas around this bitch were dropping like flies, and I had everything to do with it. I put together a team of hitters. I guaranteed niggas would feel me one way or another. A nigga had been sitting back on a situation I was trying to let my brother handle. From the look of it, nothing was getting done, so I started to feel like he was playing with me and my money, or maybe our team losing wasn't important to him.

I hated to admit it, but I wondered what was good with King. He had been acting a little off lately. I guess this shit with Lexx was real. Major was on deck, but for some reason, it was from King's angle every time we got hit. To top it off, no fucking body knew shit or gave a fuck, so it was time they did not eat until they figured it out.

I closed the shop on both sides of town to clean up, let go of all bad access, and move in the niggas who were gonna work. King was not focused, and it showed on the block and his team. Too much shit was getting by him, and I did not understand why.

I felt like King either was in on it or didn't give a fuck. Over the last five years, King had become distant. Knowing his past and how life works, I looked past it. We all had our own life outside of this dope game. We reminded each other that slipping away and getting right if needed was okay.

King was being hit too often not to notice and do something, and the same three people were on duty to get hit each time. So I cleaned up shop and set up new cameras last week. I still wanted the same niggas working for my brother on the east side to come in. One of these niggas would slip up, and I would catch it. I just had to make sure I was the only one who knew about the setup.

I walked into my club in a town called Lafayette and dapped up my workers. We all had been so busy that I forgot to make plans for my brother's birthday.

This was a last-minute thing, but I had to ensure things were still a go for the party. I had asked Chime to help get my brother there. Even though we had been through so much in the last month, I felt we could use a good night. It was their birthday, so we would bring it in with a few motherfuckers from around the way.

Outside of my workers, my brothers were all the family I had and needed. A nigga was pressed on outsiders, anyway. My trust already was fucked up, and a nigga was drained. The love I had for Lyric was gone, and the problem was knowing the truth about the past.

The sad thing was, I found out Lyric was why I got locked up. I needed to know everything about that. A nigga was on some get-back shit. I'd been on a rampage, going around killing any and every fucking body who knew something. Any time niggas on your team feel like it's okay to try you, you have to switch up the game on them to make them feel your wrath. I'd put in too much work and too many niggas on to feel unseen and unheard out here. After the streets bled, things would change. I wasn't playing.

"Yo, my friend, we good for this weekend?" I asked this gay motherfucker who worked with me to organize the party.

According to Queen, he was the best party planner in New Orleans, so I had to have him put this shit together.

"I got you, and for a good price. You trust me, yes?" His French ass asked, giving me a gay ass look. If the nigga looked at me like that one more time, I would kill him and plan this party myself. He had better get his eyes fixed.

"Okay, just send the request to my Cash App. I just texted it to you." I told him, making my way to the back of the strip club.

I had a few niggas to see before I made it home for the night. I had put a little meeting together a half-hour ago that only Major, the crew we sent to get King's team, and I knew about.

I walked in and sat down in my seat, looking at every face in front of me. They all knew me enough to understand why they were there and what time it was. I had niggas with guns at their door like a SWAT team ready to come in. All I needed to come through was Lexx. He had what I needed to put this plan in motion.

"What's going on, y'all? I'm glad y'all can make it. Sorry, we have to meet under these circumstances, but shit happens. Has anybody got the information I need?" I glanced around the room to check body language and faces. I stopped at one person who looked like he knew something. "Let's not all speak at once!" I roared.

I pulled my gun out and pointed it at Tim. He was one who I had been trying to pull off the team months ago. He looked like he had seen a ghost, and I was pleased. The nigga peed on himself. I laughed and asked this clown ass nigga, "Why are you shaking, my nigga? What's good?" He shook his head and started crying like a baby.

After standing up, I walked over to Tim. He knew what time it was, and so did the rest of them motherfuckers. I raised my gun to his head and pulled the trigger.

"Let that be a lesson to you all. I didn't have to say a word. Tim knew what he did cost him his life. Do not let it be you. Now, does anybody wanna get anything off their chest?"

"The shit I know you ain't going to like. Let me tell you in private. It's that real," my runner requested.

I dismissed everyone but him, and he proceeded to tell me what he knew.

"So, you said King set a nigga up, and he's been working with my Uncle Peanut and cousin Slime?" I asked, wanting to make sure I heard the entire story. I didn't let anybody tell me just anything. He was speaking of my blood, so he had better be on his shit.

I asked Game the name of our little lookout that nobody knew about. Major put him in the game a few months ago, so we were the only two who knew about him. The day my runner Blade got knocked off, I had to pay my respect to his family. We met his brother, Game, who knew just as much about this drug shit as I did.

The young nigga reminded me of myself when I first came out trying to make a name for myself. So far, he had blown my mind with the shit he found out and brought to my attention. I had this nigga on two sets as if he were a fly on the wall. Every time he reported back to me, he was on point. I tried not to hear what he was saying this time, hoping he was wrong. However, from what I already knew, he was on point.

I made sure I was the only one hearing what he had to say so I could play my hand right at the birthday party. "Plus, y'all boys Lexx and Dexx are twins, my gee. Man, look, I got proof of all I'm saying. I'll bring it to the party. Am I invited?" he joked. I dapped the nigga up and showed him out. I had some brainstorming to do, and fast.

∞∞∞

I was on my way home to Chime. Shawty was my safe place. I let her know I needed that body. Pulling out my phone, I texted her to make sure she did what I said. Seconds after I sent the text, she called my phone. I requested FaceTime and her beautiful face came across the screen, causing my dick to get hard.

"You gotta see this shit in person," Chime said, sounding sexy as fuck. Her ass was butt-ass naked, waiting on me.

"I'm on the way, trust me. Let me speak to my wife. I miss her," I stressed.

Chime got up, took the phone, and walked off with it. I could see her placing the phone on the bed. I smiled because she was about to blow my mind. She sat in front of the camera with her legs wide open, which was just what I wanted. She knew daddy wanted to talk to that pussy.

"Bring her closer to a nigga. She can't see daddy," I coached.

Chime positioned the phone in front of her pussy.

I was happy as fuck as I pulled my dick from my pants and wiggled it. "Open her lips wide for me," I directed, and she did just that. I spoke to my wife the whole way home. She also played with that pussy until I stepped in the door. As soon as I saw her, I fucked her ass to sleep.

Chapter Sixteen

King

My brother and I were having a small get-together, but it looked like we brought the whole state out. Shit was crazy, and there was mad love in the house tonight. I was dressed in my new fit my wardrobe assistant put me in while I was getting some head.

She knew how a nigga liked to look, so she would get a reward for it later. In Gucci from head to toe, including my shades, I was flexing on these niggas. Everyone who got the invite knew the theme was Gucci. That was my twin and me all day, plus motherfuckers called us them Gucci twins in the hood.

As soon as we walked in, I noticed the room filled with red and green Gucci balloons. One side of the room was red, Major's favorite color. The other was green, my favorite color. Niggas knew how those Gucci boys were coming before we got there. Tonight, we all needed this time together to have fun but, on the real, shit would blow up in my face if I didn't do anything to make things right.

I was too far gone and could not take back what I had already done. I was face-to-face with my brothers, and little did they know this might be their last deal. Pissing these niggas off was the least of my problems. Since Prince and Major wanted to send niggas to my spot, I would make shit shake for them. It was not like I needed them new niggas. So, since Prince changed up, would I?

I would give them all something to remember me by since they wanted to fuck with me. Family ain't everything. Money, pussy, and drugs were nowadays. That was all it took for a motherfucker to switch up on you.

These niggas needed be gone. Since I was the closest to them and the least likely person they would expect, it had to be me. Truth be told, I had shit I wanted to do once they were out of the way.

I found my way around the room, speaking to everyone. Lexx and all of them niggas showed love. The strippers were on point. I was ready to put my tongue in somebody's baby mama's ass. I made sure I stayed away from Major and Prince. They looked to be having a good time staying in the VIP section.

I was headed out the door to use the phone when I heard Prince yelling, "King, come on. Let's take a toast. Y'all ready?"

I grabbed a glass on the way over to him. I fake smiled as the music cut off.

"I'ma make this short and sweet. Fuck both y'all twinning niggas, but nawl y'all know the vibe. I love y'all for life, good or bad," Prince said.

We took our drink to that, and Prince made his way to the back with that twin bitch. He put her ass in the game fast after her sister stole from us. I was not sure how long he thought they would last. Shawty was looking good, though. I wanted to shoot my shot, but that nigga was always around blocking somebody like hell.

I saw him walk back in without her, so I took that as my chance to get to know her. Bitches started pulling on him, saying shit in his ear, which gave me a chance to slink past him. I headed to the ladies' bathroom and walked right in, looking for her ass.

Chime jumped when she saw me. She had been eying me like she had been eying Prince all night, so I didn't know why she was acting jumpy. I wanted the same shit she gave him.

"I've been looking for your fine ass. What you get a nigga for my birthday?" I asked as she washed her hands.

She looked scared as fuck, but I did not care. I would take that little pussy if I wanted it.

"Why are you even in here and coming on to me?" she asked.

I grabbed the bitch by the back of her hair and pulled her to me. "Bitch, don't let fucking with my brother go to your head. I can change your position." I threatened her ass.

Right as she started to say something, somebody came in, and shawty raced out of the bathroom. I didn't move. A nigga was drunk as fuck, so one of these bitches was going to fuck me.

"It's my birthday. Come give a nigga some head." I ordered a random-ass bitch.

She, too, flicked me off and ran out of the bathroom. I followed right behind her, running into Prince. He looked pissed. His boo told him I wanted to fuck.

"Nigga, you lost your mind. Why are you tripping like this? She's here with me, nigga!" Prince snapped, but he was not talking about shit.

Prince was talking loudly, but I was not hearing the shit he was on. He knew better. He should not even come at me like this over a bitch. We were blood. Shit, he was just bad at picking these hoes. I did not see any harm in this. In my eyes, he was just as wrong as she was. She should never have told him. I could not believe this nigga was on that time, because I asked his bitch for some pussy.

"Look, my bad, okay. We cool?" I asked the nigga.

He looked like he wanted to cry. "Don't let it happen again." He started to walk off.

I laughed aloud.

"Fuck is funny nigga?" he barked.

"You forgave a bitch that set you up but mad at me, nigga?" I gritted, looking him up and down, ready to fight.

"No disrespect because you are older than a nigga, but you can pipe that shit down. I'm not one of these niggas in the street. We got the same blood flowing through our veins. Now when you wanna talk business like a man, you can holla at me, but other than that, I'm out." Prince said as his hoe pulled him to leave.

"That's what your problem is. You always let a bitch run your life. That is why you got problems now," I pressed. "You a grown man, but it seems like you are still a child deep down under that hype."

A crowd started gathering around us.

"Y'all break this shit up. Let's go. Why y'all niggas doing this here?" Major interjected.

"Look, lock this shit up when y'all done. We out," Prince said to Major.

"Shit, I'm out too. Kesha is at the house, and I need to be under her while we still talking. Nigga, you good to close up?" Major asked me.

I shook my head, leaving those niggas up there to talk. I returned to the main room, and niggas were already heading out, which was cool. All I wanted was one of those naked strippers. I found just the right one, flashed her some money, and she took the bait. I showed her the way to the playroom and made her wait for me there. I had to clean out the club and set all the alarms.

∞∞∞

It took all of thirty minutes, but everyone was gone. I made my way to where I had left the stripper and opened the door. She was gone. I cut the light off and did my last rounds. Since the bitch was gone, I put my plan in motion as soon as I was in a safe spot. I opened my phone and dialed 911.

"I have information on a drug operation going down this week with two well-known drug lords. Who can I speak to?" I spoke when they answered, smiling like a bitch that just paid for a tummy tuck. I waited for the line to click. That is when I knew they were recording.

I did not give a fuck. This shit could get put out there but would not come back to me with how smooth I had gotten. I used a voice changer device, so they had their work cut out to figure out who made this call.

"Yes, hello, thank you for holding. I'm Detective Dick Montclair from narcotics. Did you say you had information on the two most-wanted drug lords, by any chance?" he asked.

I tried to put a face to a detective named Dick but couldn't. The only one I knew and had pull with was Detective Davis. "Yes, on Lexx Milton and Prince Brown," I relayed aloud. I had the call on speakerphone. I was still outside the club.

Locking up, I noticed one car left out there, which belonged to Chime. I remember seeing her drive up in it. After what I did to her, I knew my brother would see to it that she went home with him. I was the only one left in the building. I made sure to be the last to leave tonight. I told them I would lock up. They thought shit was cool, and we were about to act like shit never happened. But trust me when I tell you, I was watching them all.

"So, are you willing to meet with us to wear a wire, or could you take a video? Either way, we are on board. We've been waiting years to get Prince Brown and Lexx Milton. Can I ask whom I am speaking with?" the detective asked.

I got fucked up as I swung around to see Chime watching me with tears in her eyes. What had a nigga completely blown off was her phone in her hand. It looked like she was on FaceTime, and whoever was on the phone was listening to everything I said. She flipped the phone around as I hung up the call I was on. I then saw Prince smiling into the camera.

"This what we doing, my nigga? I'm leaning back in Chime's car, watching you. Tell me this, so you were going to set me up, big bruh? It be your own family. Go ahead, baby, he's dismissed." Prince instructed, but before I could respond, Chime raised the gun in her hand and shot me, and everything went black.

To Be Continued...

WANT TO INTERACT WITH T'ANN MARIE & HER TEAM?
JOIN OUR READERS GROUPS ON FACEBOOK!
T'ANN MARIE PRESENTS: GRANDMA'S HOUSE | Facebook
T'ANN MARIE PRESENTS: GRANDMA'S HOUSE 2.0 | Facebook
WIN PRIZES, BE APART OF LIVE BOOK DISCUSSIONS & MORE!

Join Our Mailing List:

http://eepurl.com/gU81k5

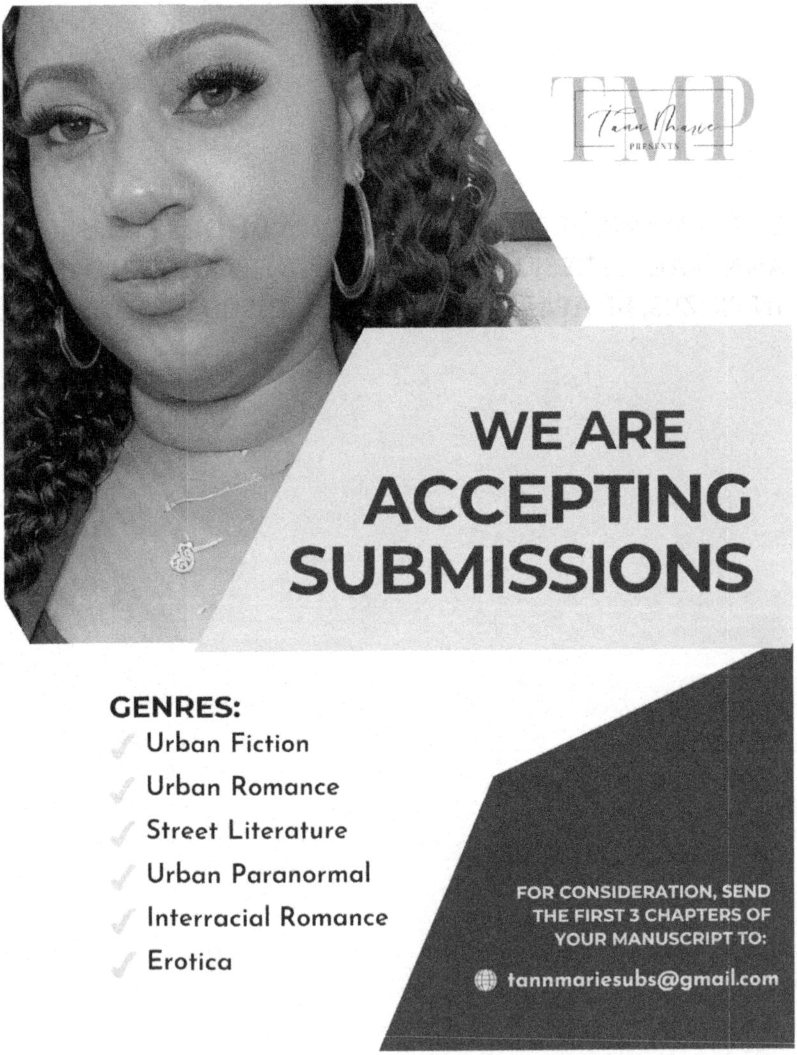